ALL ABOUT EARTHLINGS

THE IRREVERENT MUSINGS OF AN EXTRATERRESTRIAL ENVOY

∞

DECODED & TRANSLATED

BY W. E. GUTMAN

WITH AN INTRODUCTION BY WILLIAM F. WU

CCB Publishing
British Columbia, Canada

All About Earthlings:
The Irreverent Musings of an Extraterrestrial Envoy

Copyright ©2015 by W. E. Gutman
ISBN-13 978-1-77143-215-3
First Edition

Library and Archives Canada Cataloguing in Publication
Gutman, W. E., 1937-, author
All about earthlings : the irreverent musings of an extraterrestrial envoy
/ written by W. E. Gutman ; introduction by William F. Wu. -- First edition.
Issued in print and electronic formats.
ISBN 978-1-77143-215-3 (pbk.).--ISBN 978-1-77143-216-0 (pdf)
Additional cataloguing data available from Library and Archives Canada

Cover design and painting by the author.

This book is printed on acid-free paper.

Publisher: CCB Publishing
             British Columbia, Canada
             www.ccbpublishing.com

And it came to pass, when they were in the field,
that Cain rose up against Abel his brother, and slew him.
Genesis 4:8

O LORD, how long shall I cry, and thou wilt not hear!
Even cry out unto thee of violence, and thou wilt not save!
Habakkuk 1:2

Let them alone. They are blind guides of the blind;
but if a blind man leads a blind man,
both will fall into a pit.
Matthew 15:14

Also by W. E. Gutman:

JOURNEY TO XIBALBA:
The Subversion of Human Rights in Central America
Reporter's Notebook. Non-fiction. © 2000 (Out of print)

NOCTURNES -- Tales from the Dreamtime
Fiction. © 2006

FLIGHT FROM EIN SOF
Fiction. © 2009

THE INVENTOR
Historical fiction. © 2009

A PALER SHADE OF RED – Memoirs of a Radical
Autobiography. © 2012

ONE NIGHT IN COPÁN -- Chronicles of Madness Foretold
Tales of mystery, fantasy and horror. © 2012

ONE LAST DREAM
A Screenplay. © 2012

UN DERNIER RÊVE **(ONE LAST DREAM)**
Screenplay (French-language version; translated by the author).
© 2012

*What has the invention of the compass
and the discovery of faraway people done
except infect us with their maladies?*
Montesquieu (1689-1755)

*The two most common elements in the universe
are Hydrogen and stupidity.*
Harlan Ellison (1934-)

INTRODUCTION

By William F. Wu

Tick, tick, tick, tick. The Doomsday Clock is now poised at five minutes to midnight. This metaphor for the looming dangers of a civilization-threatening technological catastrophe, natural disaster or global war is the brainchild of the Bulletin of Atomic Scientists, a publication that keeps tabs on global threats, chiefly nuclear arsenals, armed conflicts, and anomalous climatic changes. Based on its findings, it determines where the clock's minute hand should rest. The nearer it is to midnight, the closer the world inches toward Armageddon.

In 1947, the clock was set at 11:53 p.m. The closest the allegorical timepiece ever came to midnight was in 1953, when the minute hand marked 11:58 p.m. following the first test of a hydrogen bomb. It was at its most optimistic in 1991, when the Cold War came to an end and the clock was set at 17 minutes to midnight. Since 1991, when it became clear that total nuclear disarmament was not in the cards, the clock has been inching again steadily toward the end times.

In January 2012, the minute hand advanced to 11:55 p.m., one minute closer to the witching hour than in 2011. The uptick was prompted by the current state of nuclear arsenals around the globe and inspired by accidents such as the Fukushima nuclear station meltdown following a major earthquake and devastating tsunami in Japan.

This year, the Bulletin chose not to ease up on its warnings of doomsday. Global instability, widening armed conflicts and environmental degradation have kept the watchdog organization in a state of nervous vigilance. It is also wary of the chill between the U.S. and Russia, two countries bristling with nuclear and other weapons of mass destruction, both tacitly committed to first-strike options. Efforts to combat climate change have also stalled. The U.S., European Union, and Australia have all wavered in their commitment to renewable energy, and Japan has backed off promises to voluntarily reduce greenhouse gas emissions. Meanwhile, China emits more of the greenhouse gases than the two biggest carbon polluters—the U.S. and India—combined, with the rate of emission soaring by about ten percent per year.

The dualistic nature of technology suggests that while it can do great things—create new sources of clean energy, help diagnose and cure diseases, enhance and lengthen life, it has been and will continue to be routinely used for evil purposes. Humans have always harnessed technology and also have been tempted and driven by it. From the time fire was controlled, people could use it to cook their food and to burn down their enemies' homes. That kind of choice endures.

As the clock ticks, veteran journalist and author W. E. Gutman believes seconds, not minutes, separate existence from extinction. In his newest and most chilling dystopia, Gutman argues that "Earthlings" will not willingly renounce war as a means of settling disputes arising from the accidental or deliberate misapplication of technology. Nor will they help ease tensions magnified by mounting doctrinal differences, overpopulation and the social and economic upheavals they engender. Instead, driven by what he calls "*a headlong freneti-*

cism, a time-shrinking haste to experience, possess, exploit, and ultimately destroy what they deem to be life's rightful rewards," Earthlings are itching for a fight and stand poised to leap into an abyss of their own creation.

ALL ABOUT EARTHLINGS, in which the author reprises themes surveyed in his other books, is a work of hyper-realism oscillating between parody, parable, and misanthropic diatribe. The historical retrospectives that undergird his narrative and the apocalyptic inferences they evoke prompt Gutman to conclude that humans are neither able nor willing to control their collective destinies: Greedy, hedonistic and reckless, they are engrossed in the here-and-now of their personal lives. Scouring through humankind's most sordid chronicles of cruelty and hypocrisy, corruption and apathy, suffering, despair and death, and extrapolating from the lessons they impart, the author envisions a scenario of otherworldly retribution that seems as fitting as it is horrible to contemplate. His use of a science fiction device (he doesn't maroon Earthlings on some faraway planet; instead, he transports an alien emissary to Earth and gives him a voice) only tends to harden the sinister nature of his auguries. Gutman takes on and unapologetically slays some mighty sacred cows in the process: God; religion; the papacy; evangelism; imperialism; militarism; capitalism; corporatism; mercantilism, and consumerism, all of which, he reckons, incestuously conspire against peace and tranquility on Earth and which, should Earth survive the evils their combined influences wreak, could one day spread beyond its celestial frontiers. Prophetic, disquieting, ferocious, and stripped of its storied trappings, ALL ABOUT EARTHLINGS is the eye that ogles itself as the clock keeps ticking. What it sees is what it gets.

Reader discretion is advised.

Nominated for the Hugo, Nebula, World Fantasy and Aurora Awards, William F. Wu is a Chinese-American scholar and science-fiction writer. He has published over a dozen novels as well as over 60 short stories. His work has appeared in a wide variety of magazines and anthologies, including OMNI Magazine and the best-selling 1996 STAR WARS: Tales from Jabba's Palace. His story "Wong's Lost and Found Emporium" was adapted into an episode of "The Twilight Zone" in 1985 and is available in the DVD set.

INTERGALACTIC SECURITY ALLIANCE

UNIVERSAL PROCLAMATION

PREAMBLE

WHEREAS it is the Intergalactic Security Alliance's mission to ensure that amity and harmony reign across the cosmos and that covenants between parties adhering to them be forthright in their efforts to secure them, and;

WHEREAS Alliance members abhor conquest, enslavement, hegemonic entrapment and economic exploitation, and;

WHEREAS secret treaties that serve private interests, are likely—should vigilance wane—to threaten civilizational bonds, and;

WHEREAS wars have been waged (some to "end all wars,") that fomented greater hostility and ignited fresh and increasingly deadly conflicts, and;

WHEREAS rational and enlightened creatures must endeavor to make our worlds fit to live in so that they may manage their existence, chart their destinies, and be assured of justice and fair dealing by the other beings of the cosmos as against force and selfish aggression, and;

WHEREAS it is not whether a majority of beings in a majority of worlds are likely to be attached to and able to secure their own liberties … but whether a majority of beings on *every* world are so attached to the principles of freedom and justice as to be as eager to defend the liberties of others as their own, and;

WHEREAS the Alliance believes that beings with distinct histories and identities can live together, and that diversity enriches societies, and;

WHEREAS members of the Alliance consider ourselves citizens of the multiverse rather than tenants of a particular biosphere; that we accept, foster and uphold the concept of *globalhood*; and that we are all in effect partners in this quest, and;

WHEREAS injustice done to one is injustice done to all, we, members of the Intergalactic Security Alliance, do hereby exhort our fellow beings to sign, ratify, and implement the Alliance's ten-point charter:

I

Covenants of peace shall be arrived at openly, after which there shall be no unilateral interplanetary understanding of any kind but diplomacy shall proceed always frankly and in the public view.

II

Absolute freedom of interstellar navigation outside planetary space boundaries shall be respected, except as segments of space may be closed, in whole or in part, as a means of enforcing the general terms of this covenant and more specifically Article **IX** below.

III

Civilization is an organism that can be in part defined by how it creates, consumes, transforms and disposes of energy. As a precondition for affiliation, and pursuant to the terms of the Alliance's science-transfer initiative, new members shall adopt, free of charge and with full assistance from our experts, technologies that render fossil fuels and other environmentally degrading or hazardous sources of energy, including nuclear power, obsolete. New members shall be given ample time to phase out coal quarrying, induced hydraulic fracturing, underground and offshore gas and oil drilling, refining and storage of products derived therefrom. Planets that refuse to suspend the processing of hydrocarbons and the manufacture of plastics, fibers, solvents, explosives and industrial chemicals for the sole purpose of protecting the industries engaged in their development and sale shall be denied membership.

IV

Adequate guarantees must be given, with regular on-site inspections, that weapons of mass destruction and precursor weapons-grade materials essential to their development and deployment shall be destroyed. The Alliance abhors the double standard, deeply entrenched in today's cosmic order, whereby certain societies claim a "right" to possess nuclear arms while simultaneously feigning moral outrage toward those who aim to acquire them. Several planets still cling firmly to these ghastly instruments of terror, believing, paradoxically, if not disingenuously, that by threatening to obliterate others they are promoting peace. By stigmatizing nuclear, biological and chemical weapons — as well as those who possess them — we can build tremendous pressure for total disarmament. A world freed of such arms will be a freer world for all.

V

A transparent and impartial adjustment of all grievances between members shall be overseen and adjudicated by the Alliance's Arbitration Board.

VI

Lest the whole structure and validity of interplanetary law and harmony be forever impaired, coercive indoctrination designed to weaken a society's sense of self-possession or subvert its independence; and cultic or dogma-driven "reeducation" schemes that exploit existential anxieties by fostering tribalism, by anchoring individuals to antediluvian beliefs, by making a virtue out of blind faith, by promoting fatalism, and by diverting generosity and good intentions for the benefit and enrichment of religious institutions violate the aims of the Alliance and will result in the immediate expulsion therefrom and the imposition of severe sanctions.

VII

Land borders, stratospheric boundaries and space frontiers capriciously carved by trespassers or expediently drawn to satisfy insular political objectives shall be readjusted along clearly recognizable lines of demarcation agreed upon through plebiscites whose results reflect recognizable cultural, ethnic and linguistic entities, as well as the aspirations of the many while not impinging on the inalienable rights of the few.

VIII

Regional associations shall be formed under specific covenants for the purpose of affording mutual guarantees of legitimate doctrinal independence and territorial integrity to great and small cosmic boroughs alike. We cannot be separated in interest or divided in purpose.

IX

Alliance members who violate the covenants to which they are bound shall be expelled and will forfeit all benefits, subsidies and compensations accorded them under Alliance rules.

X

The Alliance pledges to support free civilizations that are resisting attempted subjugation by armed internal minorities, including religious fanatics, or exoplanetary intruders. Acts of aggression against any member in good standing shall be regarded as injurious to the Alliance as a whole and will be met with swift and severe retaliatory action. Would-be members, especially those whose various factions refuse to settle differences peaceably, but whose actions, through political blackmail, annexation, exploitation and war, contribute to global insecurity, shall, after due and diligent counsel, be obliterated.

TRANSLATOR'S NOTE

I don't believe in miracles or in their polar opposites, only in coincidence, accident and synchronicity. What I am certain of is the inevitability of random events. The question is: Which events stem from chance, and which can be traced to some determinable causality, say, premeditation? Take the astonishing document that follows. Did it carelessly embed itself in my PC? Was it junk mail of the most sordid kind or did I stumble on a secure encryption that begged to be deciphered? Is this the work of a madman, a mystic, an agitator or a fiendish jokester? Is it allegory, polemic, sardonic tract or unalloyed confabulation? Or are these the mournful musings of an interplanetary onlooker, a candid account that strayed more by happenstance than scheme through the cosmic microwave background and mysteriously grafted itself onto my domain?

As there are no known crypto-detection processes capable of solving one-time ciphered communications, especially those ostensibly generated by an advanced extra-terrestrial civilization, could it be that its author chose me, an obscure and controversial reporter (and former Navy cryptanalyst), to decode and air his prophetic visions?

When serendipity can be ruled out as the source of inexplicable events, all that's left is evidence of intent. Considering his probable fluency in Earth's major idioms, the method the author of *ALL ABOUT EARTHLINGS* used to digitize and transmit his document strongly suggests that he aimed his gloomy forecasts at "Earthlings." He wanted us to know how his own kind perceives our world, what baffling image we project, what fears we arouse, and how close we are, in the cosmic scheme of things, to a violent and irreversible demise.

Cracking codes is a daunting task that poses countless challenges. First, I had to make sure that the author had not used quantum cryptography, which is currently indecipherable. He hadn't. To ensure secrecy, codes are often "super-enciphered;" they are peppered with superfluous or nonsensical additives designed to frustrate decrypting. I found no evidence of such deception.

I began with a search of symbol frequency, often-used lexes and typical groupings of terms. Other than random references by the author to an unknown home planet he calls "Yaxkin" and several entries that seem to originate from various sites around the globe, I could not tell whether the document was transmitted from Earth or from the depths of cosmic time. Finally, I had to determine whether the author had encrypted the text from a live or extinct Earth language. It wasn't. Decoded and converted into the Latin alphabet, the transcript met no known linguistic criteria; it bore no resemblance, not even remote, to any of Earth's major families of languages and dialects. Human lips, tongue, palate and larynx, I also concluded, would be incapable of articulating this language in its original form.

The most daunting challenge I faced was semantic. Despite the author's uncanny grasp of human nature, I detected terms, colloquialisms and abstractions that revealed subtle but obvious perceptual, cultural and psychological differences between his ecosphere and ours. These anomalies, which suggest a Type II civilization on the Kardashev scale — very possibly a Type III — would have baffled readers had I not extrapolated from their meaning and converted them into familiar concepts and human-friendly language.[1] In so doing, regretfully, much of the verve and lyricism that suffuse the original text were hopelessly lost in translation.

Interspersed throughout the text, readers will find occasional *[bracketed]* clauses this writer has inserted to add clarity, to simplify ambiguous concepts, to underline the obvious and, when the urge to do so became irresistible, to insinuate brief personal parenthetical remarks. I offer no apologies for this inelegant ploy. I doubt the author of this manifesto will object.

ALL ABOUT EARTHLINGS can alternately be read as a denunciation, a dirge, a harangue, an admonition, a dark oracle or a primer, an elementary overview of a virtual world to be. Its message is clear. The author — Khibxk[2] — holds a mirror in which the totality of human history is reflected. The spirited, often ferocious wit that suffuses his observations is evidence of an astute being singularly well positioned to pity or mock humankind. He warns the peoples of Earth that unless they see themselves as they are being perceived from afar and are struck with horror by the image their reflection returns, they will self-destruct or face annihilation from the great beyond.

---

[1] *The Kardashev scale of extraterrestrial civilizations was developed by Soviet Astronomer Nikolai Kardashev in 1964. It distinguishes between extraterrestrial civilizations based on their ability to harness different types of energy at a macro scale. A Type I civilization harnesses energy at the planetary level, a Type II draws energy from its sun, while Type III civilizations use galactic level energies. The November 2, 2014 video of a moon-sized UFO zooming by the Sun may be evidence that Earth's solar system is being visited by very advanced extraterrestrial civilizations that can harness the sun's plasma energy.* (Translator)

[2] *This is an approximate pronunciation.* (Translator)

WE DO NOT MAKE WAR—Call me Khibxk. Press back of tongue against uvula, bring lips together, thrust chin forward and exhale. *Khibxk*. I live on Yaxkin. Mine is not a large planet. It is not a small planet. Our mountains do not tower like those of Uaxkaklahkunx above cerulean plains nor are our seas the deepest this side of Xixmixk. Yaxkin is not blessed with Mkuluxk's paradisiacal climate nor is it cursed with Xkotzk's infernal extremes. We rise to emerald-fingered dawns and retire when crimson clouds turn to onyx. Our daylight skies are awash with pink, a hue we associate with compassion, tenderness, the innocence of childhood, the scent of love, and the timbre and texture of social justice. What makes Yaxkin exceptional is not the breadth of its cream-colored cities, the spacious tree-lined arteries that link them, the Olympian libraries, playhouses and arts centers, the wooded parks where we gather to learn, relax and revel in the gifts of creativity and genius. Our cultural institutions are publicly funded and free: We regard the humanities the preserve of the state; they are incompatible with commerce or the profit motive. We take unspoken comfort in our strength and the combined assets of our planetary allies but we do not gloat over the weakness of others or exult in their imperfections. We revere knowledge, not might. We cultivate and reward talent, not force. We cherish the communal structures we have erected and uphold

1

the compacts framed to respond to the longings and existential needs of our peers. We are at ease with ourselves. Mindful that the least religious civilizations tend to be the most peaceful, prosperous and equitable, we have long dissociated spirituality from religion which, history teaches, enflames passions, kindles hatred, and leads to bloody conflicts. We have abandoned the pretense that an invisible, mute and unknowable spirit orchestrates our lives and calls on us to account for our deeds. As Tgkunkulx Wkgakx, Yaxkin's greatest thinker said more than three millennia ago, *"Gkruxg bkaw ekhuxk mgblgk."* (A "God" who takes sides is on nobody's side).

We do not make war.

I transited on Etzknabk, our forward outpost, ten light-days into my epic journey to Earth. A briefing by our legate, Ahkauk Bkuluxk, is scheduled for the next two diurnal phases. I shall then proceed to my final destination where I am to take up my duties as one of twelve roving Intergalactic Security Alliance observers. Our mission is two-fold: One, assess Earth's capacity and readiness to join our growing family of peace-loving worlds; and two, should our findings prove encouraging, urge Earth's leaders to sign and ratify the ten-point charter in which the Alliance's ideals, objectives and statutes are enshrined.

I am less than optimistic.

I arrived on Etzknabk early in the morning on a desolate stretch of the Khayabk Plateau in the shadow of cloud-ringed Mount Xkulk. Violent squalls of swirling xenon trioxide delayed final quantum teleportation.

As I alit on the dusty plain, I peered beyond the pockmark-ed outcroppings, through rising gales of pelting amethyst-speckled sand. A crumpled terrain the color of anger stretched before me. Its disfigured visage split into winding trenches that looked like dry riverbeds. Here and there, jagged chunks of nickel-iron and iridium protruded from the surface. Dihydrogen monoxide, if it ever existed, has either long since vaporized or is now permanently frozen and trapped deep beneath the ground. To the east, the sky assumed a rich brassy copper hue. Farther south it took on a ruddy color. Another storm was fast approaching. Brooding at first, it erupted with untold fury as invisible vortices clawed at the tortured landscape and obscured it from view. The tempest of coarse glassy sand particles died down as suddenly as it had begun and glittering plumes of cosmic rays faded away as if erased by some giant hand. Temperatures plummeted to minus 130 degrees Celsius. Then, a frozen silence echoed in my ears.

Daybreak, my first on alien soil in 50 Earth years, filled me with a strange and heretofore unfelt emotion—a sharp longing for my beloved Yaxkin. I'd been warned: Prolonged deep-space journeys can short-circuit sensitivity resistors and temporarily weaken the emotive defenses of super-centenarian exogalactic travellers. I am, after all, one hundred and fifty-eight Earth years old. "Middle age" has its downside.

Remote, aloof, no bigger than the moonlit eye of a prairie wolf, the rising twin suns set Chuxkwen Peak's barren ridges afire, sending a kaleidoscopic scattering of emerald, ochre and blood-red spangles into the thin golden sky. Wispy contrails of ice crystals levitated against the blackness of space. How very strange for a lifeless planet to be arrayed in vestments of such daunting beauty.

I shut my eyes for a moment but a star-studded canopy spread out against my closed eyelids. This is Etzknabk or else I must be dreaming. Only in a dream can the folly, the arrogance, the deceptive face of reality seem so vivid, so inescapable. Etzknabk? I might as well have journeyed to

Mkuluxk or mighty Chikchkan or enigmatic Zkotzk or self-effacing Tz'kam, or some other celestial neighborhood, undiscovered, unsuspected, barely imagined, not unlike the uncharted regions of the soul.

Damn the metaphors. I, who always took pride in the clarity of my cognitive powers, I now drown in a vortex of sensations forever crippled by the meagerness of words. The circuits in my brain are overloaded. My neurons need rest; my synapses — rebooting.

A VERY ORDINARY, DIMINUTIVE STAR—Three solar cycles ago, on the first day of winter—December 21—Earth's star, the Sun, aligned with the plane of the "Milky Way" galaxy. At its center, the titanic churning black hole was as black and bottomless as ever. Earth's magnetic field had not changed. That month, the only chronicled calamities echoed man's ferocity and nature's brutish indifference to man: North Korea launched a satellite; a jittery U.S. feared that the self-isolated state aimed to develop an intercontinental ballistic missile. More than 20 people were injured during violent clashes in Mexico City. The Taliban attacked a NATO airstrip in Eastern Afghanistan. Islamist fighters went on a rampage in Nigeria, hacking ten Christians to death with machetes. Typhoon Bopha slammed into the Philippines, killing more than 1,000 people. In Northern Ireland, 15 police officers were injured during a riot at the Belfast City Hall. The U.S. refused to ratify the United Nations Convention on the Rights of Persons with Disabilities. Violent clashes erupted in Bangladesh. Toutatis 4179, an asteroid about three miles wide passed within 4.3 million miles (or 18 lunar distances) of Earth. Japan scrambled fighter jets in response to a Chinese warplane seen near the disputed Senkaku Islands. A shooting at Sandy Hook Elementary School in Newtown, Connecticut, left 28 people dead, including 20 children. A man in China attacked an elderly woman with her own knife then stabbed 22 children. Taliban gunmen killed six health workers in Pakistan. Despite worldwide criticism, Israel pressed on with the construction of thousands of new homes on occupied Palestinian lands in the West Bank and East Jerusalem. At least 40 people were killed in clashes between rival communities in Kenya. A severe cold spell killed 85 people in Ukraine, 45 in Russia. Police in China arrested 1,000 people belonging to the doomsday Almighty God Christian cult for spreading rumors about the "Endtime."

Apocalypse had been big business for 2,000 Earth years or more. From ancient Persia to Daniel and Enoch and Habakkuk and Ezekiel and the deranged author of Revelation and the death-obsessed Mayan chronicles, deceivers and impostors and self-deluded mystics had hoodwinked the multitudes and driven them to lunacy.

As I journeyed from Yaxkin, I told myself that future explorers, however vast their knowledge might be, will bear burdens of ignorance immensely heavier than my own. But once aloft, their sails will hug the wind and ride the tempest. For, they too shall have dared to go beyond their dreams as prophets of doom, foiled again, rewrite their contemptible scripts.

How do I paint a point in space? How do I behold the face of Kakbkan? By surrendering to sightless, speechless cogitation? It is the very nature of such journeys that compels those of us who embark on their gossamer wings to question their significance or merit. What's the point? We are apt to discover on arrival at some unscheduled port of call, as I did on Etzknabk's barren escarpments, then on Earth's blood-splattered shores, that there may have been no good reason to make the trek in the first place. For when all is said and done, at the very end of some aimless peregrination, worn out and confused, we might sadly conclude that the farthest point in space is just too dangerously close, just not meant to be.

∞

Bent by gravity, distorted by cosmic rays and electromagnetic pulses, sounds of euphoria, distant, almost alien, soon began to crackle through my headset. It was Yaxkin, home sweet home. I first heard thunderous applause then the coalescing encomiums of family and friends who had gathered around the visual display unit. Bone-tired, listless, I acknowledged their jubilant cheers perhaps more tersely than I'd intended. I asked for everyone's indulgence; I was exhausted. I turned off the transmitter and ran through the debarkation protocols.

What I glimpsed of Earth can best be told in pictures. Image catchers [*cameras*] have no soul, just eyes. That's what keeps them honest. They will record with poetic unconcern, as they did on my first epic voyage to "Terra" half a century ago, an awesome spectacle of hyperactivity and wasted motion, of hopeless exertion and premature entropy, of hedonism and prodigality, ostentation and appalling want, injustice and unspeakable suffering.

What I felt is less easily defined, far more prone to understatement or colossal exaggeration. Feelings, like dreams, are hard to apprehend and just as slippery. I shall not risk falsifying my emotions by parsing them just yet. This is Earth, I keep telling myself, the third planet from a very ordinary and diminutive star tucked away far from the event horizon of an unremarkable galaxy we have all been watching, agog and terrified, for millennia. This is the inexplicably trendy destination among a new wave of interplanetary vagabonds and gullible expats, and now chanced upon face to face yet again, not as the youthful adventurer I was on my maiden voyage but as an emissary. I wonder whether the travails of diplomacy are worth the sacrifice of exile from what was until a dozen light-days ago a tranquil existence on Yaxkin. I hope it shall not have been in vain. Hope is what's left when instinct and experience are ignored. It's an antidote against reality.

I come in peace. Armed with cautious hope, I shall try to jettison preconceived ideas and reassess views formed during my first visit to Earth 50 years ago. Some endeavors require a counterintuitive approach.

HELL GETS MORE CROWDED EVERY DAY—I first came to Earth as a wanderlust-smitten lad. I'd bummed a ride to Oxlakhun, *[catalogued by astronomers as a sphere in the Kepler-69 "habitable zone"]* on a veteran interplanetary freighter, the now decommissioned *Pulsar Runner*, and teleported the rest of the way. It was a rite of passage my family had reluctantly sanctioned: A few weeks on Earth, they surmised, would cure an "absurd infatuation" with a world they openly scorned, and I would promptly turn tail and head home to Yaxkin. They were right, of course, but it took longer than a few weeks. I would spend more than a decade lurching from brief states of wonderment to exasperation and unease as I attempted to fit in, hopelessly out of step, out of tune. The harder I tried to anthropomorphize, the more I became a restive stranger, uncomfortable not in my own alien skin but in everything that touched it. I was slowly mutating back to my real, unalterable self—a cosmic castaway, an interloper adrift in a realm I did not fully comprehend. Outwardly poised, inwardly raging, defiant and aching, lost in the blinding lights and sounds and frenzied kinesis of Earth, I trod unfamiliar waters; everything about Earth added to my estrangement, perplexity and homesickness.

It was winter. New York towered above me, gray, dank, otherworldly, menacing, as I shivered. I tried to make sense of this latest disembodiment. Driven by an age-old momentum, in search of new horizons, convinced that permanency can be attained only through change, I'd left Yaxkin and embarked on what I'd hoped to be a life of serene itinerancy. I found myself marooned instead on the unfriendly shores of a realm that preaches love in its houses of worship and practices hate on its streets and battlefields.

America: Industrious; affluent; smug, secure in its hypocrisy and grotesque affectations. A likable minstrel named Elvis Aaron Presley scandalized that nation's straitlaced soul with his hip-swinging hit single, *Blue Suede Shoes*, but no one objected when, fiercely opposed to racial integration, 96 members of Congress signed the *Southern Manifesto*. Nor would anyone be outraged to learn, after his death 53 years later, that Senator Strom Thurmond, the self-confessed bigot who co-authored the manifesto, had fathered a child with his black maid.

Schools, lunch counters, public lavatories and water fountains were segregated. People of color still rode at the back of the bus. They were often lynched, arrested on trumped-up charges, wrongly convicted and imprisoned, humiliated and dehumanized. Many, after spending years on death row, were executed because white justice was not, is not—can never be—color-blind. But what the hell, if your skin was white and you had a steady job, life was just a bowl of cherries.

Post-war America was economically sound, bursting with hope, brimming with opportunity. A family of four lived comfortably on one wage-earner's salary. The dollar had weight and worth. *"Made in the USA"* was a seal of excellence. A gallon of gas cost 23 cents! You could buy a decent house for $22,000. A car cost around $2,000.

One day, sensing that foreign policy is strictly about power and narrow interests [*whereas a growing conservative fringe deemed values and morals to be for the feeble-minded*] President Eisenhower warned against the "military-industrial complex" and against armed entanglements while economists and social scientists cautioned against the very excesses that, six decades later would turn the U.S. into a fascist mafia state dedicated to enriching a privileged few by impoverishing the many. If a system is built on power, but lacks legitimacy, behaviorists pleaded, it will destroy itself. If it asserts moral truths but lacks the power to enforce them, it will unravel. Their counsel fell on deaf ears.

Relaxed, playful, upbeat, frivolous, given to good-natured inanity—as witnessed by the dimwitted feel-good movies it released that decade—America soon bared its soul and hinted at the veiled anxieties, the restless self-inquiry to which it would later succumb as the world began to unravel. Hollywood turned introspective: *East of Eden. Rebel Without a Cause. The Blackboard Jungle. The Bad Seed. The Wild One. Marty. Suddenly Last Summer.* Orwell published his prescient dystopia, *1984.* They all echoed feelings of unease first articulated in the internal dialogues of a country stirring from affluence and complacency to vigilance, from presumed invincibility to perceived vulnerability, and now willing to shed its ill-fitting and deceptive disguise. But the small screen, which held the bulk of America captive, retaliated. The strong, silent, bronco-bustin' pistol-packin' cigarillo-chompin' Bourbon-chuggin' square-jawed desperados and enforcers took over. *The Rifleman, Gunsmoke, The Virginian, Maverick, Wagon Train, Rawhide, Wyatt Earp, Have Gun: Will Travel, Bonanza*—all exalted America's violent past and repackaged banditry into downhome entertainment.[3]

The Sixties ushered an era oxygenated by the rise of an ebullient counterculture. Freed from the affectations of the finicky Fifties, cleansed from the obscenity of McCarthyism, sickened by the Vietnam War, the Kent State massacre, the Watergate scandal, America welcomed the Beatles, let its hair down, burned draft cards, set the flag on fire, torched ROTC buildings and donned bell-bottom pants, Nehru jackets, dashikis and beaded necklaces. Malcolm X electrified his people and shocked white America. Black Panther leader Eldridge Cleaver and comedian Dick Gregory, the eloquent civil rights drum major, parlayed acerbic tongue and mordant wit into a brand of social activism that bolstered black America's self-identity.

Back from Paris where he had been embraced and feted, James Baldwin rose from obscurity to become a commanding figure in American literature.

Also back from France where she'd blossomed and honed an uncompromising sense of justice, Sartre scholar and one of the FBI's Ten Most Wanted Fugitives, Angela Davis, took America by storm.

A cultural phenomenon, Alex Haley's *Roots* presented for the first time a black perspective of life in Africa and unerringly recorded the bestiality of slavery. In *Kunta Kinte* were incarnated the horrors and heroism of the black experience.

Lenny Bruce, Mort Sahl and George Carlin turned humor on its head. Their irreverence and biting political satire challenged an outwardly straitlaced but dissolute society and helped redefine and broaden free speech. Jack Kerouac, the

---

[3] *The Pentagon has long influenced Hollywood. Movies that were given a "hand" include Black Hawk Down, Top Gun, Saving Private Ryan, the Right Stuff, Apollo 13 and Lone Survivor, one of this decade's goriest war-glorifying propaganda films.* (Translator)

leading chronicler of the "beat generation" *[he coined the term]* shocked America with autobiographical sketches that betrayed deep social unease assuaged by drugs, alcohol and scorching humor. His leading apostle, Allen Ginsberg, vented his rage against materialism with an angst-ridden lyricism kindled by LSD. Flower children preached love, not war. *Oh! Calcutta*, memorable for its brazen display of frontal nudity, male and female, and *Hair*, America's tribal love-rock musical, opened to rave reviews. The plays would enthrall audiences for years to come. This was an era of rebellious sex and drugs and freedom from the shackles of conformity, a time of nascent impiety and suspicion toward the political structures that Americans had taken for granted and naïvely trusted, an epoch long remembered and still reviled by the reactionaries who lived through it and died a little as liberal victories slowly changed the face of their beloved obstructionist paradise.

I watched these transformations with a relish that fostered in me an impish urge to partake. But I abstained. I inwardly rejoiced at the consternation these upheavals seemed to wreak upon America's squeamish psyche, but I espoused none of the causes they championed or spawned, at least not openly. While I can materialize at will—I prefer invisibility (molecular transparency is a scientifically more accurate term)—I did not put on a wig until long hair was passé. I took it off as soon as manes were back in vogue. I pasted on a beard when facial hair went out of style; I removed it the moment hirsute cheeks and chins outnumbered beardless ones. I adopted none of the fashions or affectations of the time—polyester leisure suits and wide psychedelic neckties and bandannas and high-heeled clogs and anti-bomb peace symbols. I used none of the jargon, neologisms, and mannerisms typical of that era. I symbolically "dropped out" in my own time, at my own pace, disinclined to assert my extra-terrestrial individuality by rushing to embrace someone else's conformist eccentricities. Purely academic, my fascination with Earth's politics of dissent remained voyeuristic. I refused to get involved for fear that doing so would compromise my spectator status and betray my origins. But I was secretly elated. For an instant, I felt that young progressives and old radicals had at last recognized the real enemy, had learned how to fight and would now be pushing for meaningful reforms. Reality trumps the most fervent expectations. When capitalism is the enemy, freethinking, enlightenment, and egalitarianism don't have a prayer.

I experimented with Tetrahydrocannabinol and its more potent trichome *[hashish]*, crude and malodorous mood-altering weeds that deliver a mediocre "high" compared to the ecstasy our euphoriatrons produce. I shunned the demented and slovenly atmosphere of pot parties. Fed up with the inane laughter, the tangential, off-the-wall dialogue, the brutish sex, the narcoleptic sleep, the Dionysian junk-food binges, I got high alone in semidarkness and utter silence, plumbing the musings, images and moods the unremarkable psychedelic visions stirred. Bored with a steady diet of "altered states," sickened by the immoderate craving for food they engendered, tired of sinking into an abyss of melancholy as the effects wore off, I gave up the weed and surrendered to wrenching longings for home.

The flower children and the anti-war activists have all since grown into flabby, self-absorbed, cynical sexagenarian loafers. They once protested injustice and chicanery, they marched against ignoble wars, they poured scorn upon shameless leaders while young Americans died far from home and lies and colossal fraud were being heaped on a nation too smug to care. Weakened by indifference or stilled by material ease, the irresolute voices of dissent, the cries for peace and justice would soon be muted.

Instead, Ronald Reagan, the "great communicator," inspired in Americans feelings of optimism-by-amnesia at the very moment that a dejected, failure-haunted nation had been poised to awaken and look at itself. Those were grim years. The horrors went beyond defeat in Vietnam and Watergate revelations of skullduggery in high places. Meat prices doubled, for no apparent reason, and an Arab oil boycott brought further inflation. There were long lines at the pump driven by artificially contrived gas shortages. Crime soared. Congress uncovered years of law-breaking and assassinations by the CIA. In a bankrupt, squalid New York City, garbage piled up in the streets. The forced integration of black and white schools set off bombings. The entire junior class at West Point was disciplined for cheating. Radical groups such as the Weather Underground mounted terror attacks from coast to coast. Americans were unnerved; they wanted to be "proud" again. But "pride," at a time when violence, scandals and debacles buffeted the U.S., concealed a hankering for the glib remedies hyped by an emerging New Right that preached an "every-man-for-himself" philosophy and sowed the seeds of fear and racial intolerance.

Nothing illustrates America's bulimic appetite for war more cynically than how it tracks, targets, psychologically remodels and draws teenagers to military recruiting offices. Hungry for new conscripts, military planners commission psychological research and carefully study neuropsychiatric literature as it pertains to adolescent behavior. They then apply their findings to their recruitment efforts that prey on the vulnerability of the immature juvenile mind.

Enlistment needs are met by investing billions of taxpayer currency units on programs designed to deceive, seduce and capture the youth of America. The Pentagon, which had long cultivated a cozy relationship with the entertainment industry, invaded the movies and television and inveigled children to play violent video games while feeding them emotionally charged content designed to influence and reformat them into compliant "patriotic" expendable replacement soldiers.

America is merrily sauntering down a primrose path of media-driven mythmaking. Corporate mainstream media organizations, the pundits they sponsor and manipulate, and politicians from both parties have composed a new contextual refrain: "On September 11, 2001, everything changed." From cable TV to AM radio, from the blogosphere to town-hall meetings, Americans are repeatedly told: "This is a post-9/11 world."

Many Americans have since surmised that "everything" did not change. Corporate media have resurrected powerful myths from America's past to shape public perception in the present. In fact, the media are doing more mythmaking than investigative reporting. Even before it became a nation, the U.S. relied heavily on cultural mythology to instill in its citizens a sense of meaning and purpose. As their needs changed, Americans told themselves new stories. They spun new myths.

∞

A monotonous downpour drenched Manhattan with chilling persistence. Broadway stretched before me, a dank canyon in which a million lights flickered through the sulfurous mist. They were all there; drunks, drifters, hawkers, doomsday prophets and reformers, the homeless and the transient, visitors and harried commuters. It was the West Side and men with upturned collars and vacant expressions walked right into me, as if I wasn't there. Creatures of all genders trapped me in their staring game and I didn't know if their eyes conveyed hatred, lust or defiance. I didn't want to miss a single nuance so I stretched my gaze to the limits of peripheral vision until I found a new pair of eyes up ahead. And the contest resumed. I remember reaching Forty Second Street, the outer rim of a funnel through which churns a backwash of humanity. The light turned red. I stopped. At my feet lay the puddles, like bottomless black lagoons in which shimmer all sorts of eerie reflections. Everything around me seemed to reinforce life's constrictions. *STOP. ONE WAY. YIELD. NO PARKING. NO STANDING. NO RIGHT TURN. NO LEFT TURN. WALK. DON'T WALK. DETOUR. DO NOT ENTER. SLOW. DEAD END.*

Grand Central Station. I remember a nun begging for alms at the bottom of a steep, interminable subway escalator. She sat on a folding chair, night after night, gazing vacantly at the hordes that spilled at her feet. She nodded, slowly, rhythmically. Her lips moved but the whirr of the escalator and the roar of the trains engulfed her incantations. She may have been reciting the rosary, the paternoster, an endless mantra of benedictions, or she may simply have been murmuring, *"Welcome to hell, welcome to hell...."*

Redemption, she knew, can be bargained for with a little kindness. The generous ones, few as they were, only gave on Fridays or holidays. The others pretended not to see her.

Underground, where commuters surrender to a numbing daily cadence—hurry to work, hurry back home—life seems thin and fitful, snatched in haste, endured with wariness in guilt-ridden anonymity by an evanescent and forever re-forming mob that barely tolerates itself. And there seems to exude from this pulsating, throbbing, scurrying mass of people a smell of hostility and fear and boredom, all of it skillfully concealed behind a million expressionless eyes.

Sooner or later, I noted, everyone made a special effort to diminish the guilt. So the nun waited. And hell got more crowded every day.

NEITHER APE NOR ANGEL—What sets Yaxkin and our Alliance partners apart from primal or up-and-coming worlds such as Earth is the gift of clairvoyance. And what makes Earthlings so unpredictable is their inability to divine the obvious.

Yet, every now and then, usually by default, and seldom on the first try, Earthlings have been known to blunder on a fact or two. Wrenched from the shadows of ignorance or chanced upon by some careless time traveler, their discoveries have often shattered deep-seated if somewhat unsustainable beliefs—that Earth is the center of the universe; that lead can be transmuted into gold; that black cats are bearers of bad luck; that Columbus "discovered" America; that meteors are "heavenly omens;" that the word "theory" implies mainstream scientific doubt about its validity; that "evolution" attempts to explain the origin of life; that humans and dinosaurs coexisted; that astrology is a science; and that "bad air" causes malaria.

It was shortly after my arrival on Earth, at a time when, for many, fate still ruled the world, when circumstance, not scheme, random chance, not purpose or plan molded Earthlings' destiny, that two camps vied for the truth; and both held it for a while.

Fat and sated like iguanas basking in the sun, wading in

and out of the primordial soup where it's cozy and warm, Darwinists made no bones about it. Their blueprint was foolproof. Evolution made sense. One by one, the pieces of the gigantic puzzle began to fit into place with such symmetry as to make some transcendental first cause — 'divine' or quantum-defined — not only probable but essential. They just didn't call it "God's" masterwork.

Miffed at Darwin's irreverence, unwilling to concede that they are descended from apes, not angels, Creationists kept invoking "Intelligent Design" — as if evolution were not in itself an astounding singularity. And life went on.

One day, for no apparent reason, cosmologists began splitting cosmic hair. With the *Big Bang vs. Steady State* debate well behind them, though still deadlocked on several core issues, they now asked each other *[and themselves, no doubt]*: Is the universe "open" or "closed?" Does intergalactic space extend indefinitely and in all directions, or do as yet undetected boundaries originating at some inscrutably distant point mark its final limits? And, if so, what lies beyond?[4]

What is space, anyway, they asked. Is it a circumstantial realm with no intrinsic dimension, no reality of its own except that which is fancied by Earthlings in their convoluted ruminations? Is space a byproduct of human consciousness, like time, which is seen as "passing" but in fact does not move? Some astrophysicists insisted that space is not only endowed with quantifiable form and volume, but that it is

---

[4] *Every Yaxkinian toddler knows that the cosmos is the offspring of nuclear fusion, not fission. The nuclei responsible for outward expansion have always existed. As they collide, they spread out ceaselessly and spawn separate and ever-expanding universes in a process known as eternal cosmic inflation. The "cosmos" is not a single four-dimensional entity but the cumulative totality of an ever-increasing number of universes. In fact, the universe has no beginning. Like infinity, this is a concept that even the brainiest Earthlings have a hard time grasping.* (Translator)

also measurable by a timeline that includes a starting point, a first cause, or alpha, but not necessarily an omega. Others retorted with disarming logic that something that has no boundaries cannot possibly have shape, surface or volume.

Surely, while these mental pirouettes severely strained the limits of consciousness, others yet agreed that infinity is the province of philosophers and mystics. After all, probes sent out on scouting missions to the farthest reaches of the inky void had gone on one-way odysseys and no one knew for sure what they would run into, or when.

For a while, the case for an open or "infinite" universe gained ground. Infinity is a tolerable abstraction because, like all absolutes, it is as self-limiting as it is unquantifiable. Something that has no shape or computable dimensions, however keenly one may try to contain it, cannot have being. Earthlings cope with inscrutability either by ignoring it or turning it into an article of faith. Sometimes ignorance is bliss, even among the learned. *[One man's bliss is generally the source of someone else's misery]*.

In time, however, unable to bolster their respective positions, scientists reached an impasse—and a compromise. It became fashionable to argue that, for lack of a more convincing explanation, perpetual space-time and cosmic confinement may be one and the same. The difference, they offered, existed in the mind's eye of poets and stargazers and dreamers and a science fiction writer or two. It was, pardon the irresistible pun, pretty much an open-and-shut case. Adding to the confusion, perhaps out of desperation, perhaps in an attempt to blur the distinction between knowledge and whimsy, an imaginative physicist suggested that reality is a hologram. Another proposed the startling idea that the fundamental ingredients of nature are inconceivably microscopic strings of energy whose inherent modes of vibration underlie everything that happens in the universe.

Someone else theorized that the universe is a figment of "God's" imagination. One of the latest theories suggests that the universe shouldn't exist at all but fails to explain why it does. And another era came and went in a cosmos unconcerned with the pitiable struggles and contests of a wretched organism that keeps breeding itself out of existence.

And then it happened, not unexpectedly perhaps, but with devastating finality:

"WE ARE ALONE!" banner headlines proclaimed from Paris to Pretoria, Moscow to Montevideo, New York to Nanjing: **"HUMANKIND: AN ACCIDENT,"** they screamed impiously on all the front pages. Carefully worded, unadorned, prosaic, aloof, spreading across the page, the article ignited passions, provoked outrage or stupor, clouded the mind, froze Earthlings' brittle spirit:

> *"An international team of astrophysicists has released details of a study which confirms that 'intelligent life' is confined to planet Earth, and that the odds of a similar biogenic manifestation occurring elsewhere in the universe are close to nil.*
>
> *"Dismissing critics charging that such view smacks of 'cosmic egocentricity,' the study recommends that the search for extraterrestrial life be halted and that efforts and assets be refocused on heretofore neglected Earthbound priorities such as overpopulation, climate change, dwindling natural resources, poverty, hunger and disease.*
>
> *"Drafted by the Yearly Astrophysical Heliotropic Watch Experiment in Hyperspace, the 2,000-page document asserts that, 'life is the aftermath of a spontaneous and unrepeatable paradox,' and that humankind, is 'an experiment gone wrong.'*
>
> *"Alluding to Albert Einstein's celebrated but misconstrued rebuff, 'God does not play dice with the universe,' a spokesman said that 'God had indeed gambled when He fashioned the*

universe — and lost. Perched atop a speck of dust in the limitless void,' the study concluded, 'aided by providence and propelled by natural selection, the human race is an occurrence — an accident — the result of an endless succession of unpremeditated chance events, all of which continue to unfold as we travel through time.'

"*Supporting the study's conclusions, a joint communiqué issued by the world's spiritual leaders upheld the scientific findings. In an extraordinary gesture of humility and conciliation, quoting Boethius — 'As far as you are able, join faith to reason' — the communiqué conceded that 'God, the epitome of perfection,' had let His imagination run wild when He fashioned humans, and that unlike humans who never seem to learn from past mistakes, 'He had been mindful not to repeat such abomination elsewhere in His dominion'.*"

Little did Earthlings know that while imaginary creatures populated their dreams, super-intelligent "biogenic manifestations" inhabiting wide swatches of intergalactic space looked on in horror and wept at the images their inferences evoked.

THE NEW WORLD HOARDER—No, America is not a monolith. Viewed from a distance, however, it matches the caricature-like image many Earthlings and members of the Intergalactic Security Alliance have formed. Of America, which forswore all princes and potentates in exchange for the majesty of self-rule *[but capitulated to the czars of capital]* I quickly distilled a theocentric nation hooked on triumphalism, given to gluttonous mercantilism and bulimic consumerism, a colossus beguiled by its grandiose self-view and readily seduced by the idolatrous slogans it keeps coining in its own name; a titan obsessed with bigness: Super-sized meals; wall-sized televisions; monster trucks; jumbo jets; mammoth multistoried seafaring pleasure vessels; behemoth churches.

Of Americans, I deduced a sanguine, gregarious and resourceful people foolishly prone to frivolity and hero-worship. No, they do not revere Einstein or Freud, Galileo or Mark Twain, the Dalai Lama or Abraham Lincoln, Beethoven, Shakespeare, Albert Schweitzer or Michelangelo. Instead they deify thespians and troubadours *[many of dubious talent]*, fictional übermenschen, comely people and sports figures, most of them mediocre human beings who but for their height or brawn or dexterity with some implement, such as a ball, a club, a stick or a pair of boxing gloves, would be picking up garbage or draining septic tanks instead of earning obscene wages.

At their best, Americans are probably the most generous people on Earth. At their worst, I found them to be annoyingly provincial, bigoted, outwardly cocksure, inwardly skittish, overindulged, overfed, and oversexed. The men are high-strung, driven, homophobic, sexually conflicted. Bursting with testosterone, they are desperately protective of their masculinity, enamored of their cars and enraptured by their guns which they keep oiled, loaded, and cocked. I found their women prematurely pubertal and, as they age, increasingly neurotic and ornery. Both genders seem to be in awe of status symbols; both are deaf or hostile to unorthodox ideas. Owing genomic and temperamental differences — I being a hopelessly rational Yaxkinian — Earthlings and I can never hope to entertain a meaningful relationship.

To those who suggest that America has changed in the past 50 years, I submit that it is just more *revealed*: It was always a charismatic fraudster; it finally bared its vulgar soul when Barack Hussein Obama ran for president, was elected, and then reelected for a second term. Who can forget protest signs showing a white-faced and blood-mouthed Obama as a satanic clown image, or his portrayal as Hitler, complete with mustache and swastika? How odd that burning the flag infuriates Americans, but depicting the president as a clown and a maniacal fascist is a legitimate expression of "free speech."

The ugly aftershocks and secessionist rants that Obama's victories generated, the deep current of racism coursing through America's veins, suggest that at least half of America's electorate is bigoted, xenophobic, anti-progressive, homophobic, misogynous, and dementedly religious.

[The November 2014 mid-term elections, in which six of the most backsliding states helped Republicans regain control of the

Senate, tend to validate that premise]. Had Obama lost the elections, I would have concluded that most Americans are just dim-witted and mean-spirited. But in America's first black commander in chief, they now saw a symbol of that nation's increasing diversity and "change" that scared them. The potential for racially motivated violence was never higher. Americans don't like to be reminded of their shortcomings. So I keep my opinions to myself.

∞

Chinks are developing in the American bubble. The more perspicacious Americans are beginning to note, with some unease, that the U.S. does not *[and never actually did]* resemble the mythical image it has of itself except perhaps in the grand and illusory dreams of the so-called Founding Fathers. The U.S. has since turned into an opportunistic, self-indulgent, arrogant and sanctimonious empire now headed for a tightly controlled *[spied on]* feudal society consisting of small groups of immensely rich lords and increasingly larger castes of serfs doomed to a life of bondage. While it retains the trappings of a liberal democracy, with an elected body of legislators and perfunctory elections, its institutions are alarmingly hollow and corruptible, and their power springs from corporate elites. America is jumpy, angry, violent and morally bankrupt. More and more Americans are struggling to survive and, as a number of socio-economic indicators foretell, they will face even harder times ahead.

Given my Yaxkinian tendency to compare, and seen through the prism of relativity, my analysis of America is not one in which I take pleasure. Alas, as time passes I find more evidence to support it. If America only abandoned its pretenses and conceded that it is not the "leader of the free world;" that its concept of "liberty and justice for all" is a sham, that during its gestation and after its birth as a nation it engaged in ruthless acts of banditry, first against Mother England, against native populations which it nearly liquidated and the imported "labor" which it enslaved for more than two centuries, then in wars of imperialistic expansion and economic colonialism; that its wealth is based on merciless capitalism and the worship of privileged classes—then I would say, OK, the problem is not America per se, it's Earthlings. But when a nation goes to such lengths to proclaim its invincibility, to trumpet its moral superiority, to vaunt its puritanism *[as it wallows in shameless promiscuity]*, when it pompously grants itself the right to teach the rest of the world how to behave, when it meddles in other people's affairs in the name of "national security," when it ships the flower of its youth to die, be maimed or rendered insane in illegal, immoral and unwinnable wars, then it's not Earthlings anymore, it's a national state of mind, a mentality, an attitude, a unique societal trait. A superpower that professes moral arguments to buttress its global vision for civil liberties and democracy cannot just abandon those standards in its senseless search for absolute security.

One must be extraordinarily rich in America to protect one's assets. The average worker can barely keep his head above water and the taxation system makes sure he can never climb out of it. Every dollar he puts in a savings account has already been taxed. Why is he being taxed a second time for conducting what is essentially a private transaction between himself and a depository? Why are his earnings assessed when some corporations pay no taxes at all? Why do corporate executives receive millions of dollars in yearly bonuses and the steel worker who erects skyscrapers has zero say in how his tax dollars are being spent? Why are there no dollar reserves to fund cultural institutions, build schools and feed the poor but plenty of money to wage war and keep hundreds of thousands of American troops stationed around the world?

The U.S. has the highest rate of poverty among industrial nations. There are one million homeless minors. It ranks 37 in health care—after tiny Costa Rica *[France is still No. 1]*. It warehouses the largest prison population in the world and has turned incarceration into a business largely sustained by minorities. The death penalty is still in effect in thirty-five states. Had it not been for President Lyndon B. Johnson's bold *[and reviled]* Civil Rights Act of 1964, Jim Crow would still be king *[as he is in some southern cantons]*. There were some 13,000 gun-related deaths in America in 2012—only 50 in France and the U.K. The U.S. is the only Western nation where "God" is allowed to muscle in on the body politic. Once a leader in the humanities, it has since cut funds to education, the arts, music. Mindless forms of television programming are being increasingly directed at rural audiences. America's infrastructure is crumbling: Roads and bridges are in a state of shocking disrepair; schools, hospitals, mental institutions are closing at an alarming rate *[but prisons are bursting at the seams]*. There are four times more high school dropouts than in 1956, when I first came to Earth, and those who graduate can't spell. Math grades continue to drop. A climate of anti-intellectualism, anti-erudition prevails. America's love affair with guns is a form of osmotic psychosis unrelated to an ill-conceived 18th century statute that has since been hijacked by the gun lobby and sanctified by low-brow Goths. What is it about their temperament that convinces Americans they are entitled to own guns? Surely it's not the poorly-worded and nearsighted codicil penned some 230 years ago. A failure at its conception, aimed at safeguarding medieval rights, the

Second Amendment continues to be summoned by extremists who call themselves conservatives and who are more interested in commerce and private ownership than egalitarianism (or personal safety).

∞

Yaxkinians have lots of questions. The answers, we believe, are axiomatic, self-evident and consistent with our observations. We are not as upbeat about America as some Americans seem to be. We agonize over the inherent weakness of "democracy." Sooner or later, any system that allows in its bosom the birth, existence, and propagation of anti-democratic institutions is bound to fail.

∞

I don't have to revisit the Crusades, the St. Bartholomew massacre, the Inquisition, the Thirty-Years' War, the centuries-old sectarian strife in Ireland, the Armenian and Jewish Holocausts, the Hutu-Tutsi reciprocal slaughter, the Hindu-Muslim conflict in India and Kashmir, the bloodbath in Sudan and the endless Shia-Sunni carnage. All I have to do is look at the United States, at the proliferating dynasties of Elmer Gantries who commandeer America's psyche *[while rifling through its pockets]*, at imbeciles who equate environmentalism with totalitarianism and the loss of individual freedom, at anti-government "Patriot" activists whose fears are rooted in right-wing lore about the emergence of a New World Order—in short at a maniacal, snarling phalanx of soul-robbers—to find all the raw materials that coalesce into intolerance, cruelty and lunacy.

Americans know who they are. They should; they've been told and retold by their parents, teachers, politicians, and "spiritual advisors" that America is:

• The world's most formidable military power *[it lost in Korea, Indochina Somalia, and Iraq; it "won" against tiny Grenada and Panama...]*; it is being held hostage in Afghanistan, Iraq and Syria. A stalemate is always worse than defeat.

• The guarantor of democracy *[the U.S. trails Norway, Iceland, Denmark, Sweden, New Zealand and Australia]*.

• The beacon of spiritual impartiality *[while abetting the incestuous tryst between the body politic and the dinosaurs of the religious right]*.

• A paragon of puritan chastity *[it is awash in vice]*.

• A model of equity *[Americans denounce abortion but cheer when a condemned man is hanged, roasted, or injected with a lethal cocktail of drugs]*.

• The guardian of a free press *[an increasingly faint-hearted, formulaic mainstream media that won't challenge the evisceration of civil liberties; the enfeeblement of the middle class; the consolidation of wealth into ever-narrower circles of power; unemployment; racism; the offensive against labor; the soaring price of food and medicines; the predatory healthcare system; and the staggering cost of environmental degradation]*.

America is a nation of superlatives. Obsessed with bigness, Americans want more and, darn it, they'll elect the people who promise to deliver. In politics, posture is everything; to hell with character or substance. Americans are fond of histrionics. They thrive on the dazzling displays of dirt-flinging and farcicalities regurgitated before major elections. Seen by the foreign press, the circus to which they are treated every four years adds yet another dimension to the national character: A puerile taste for fatuity.

"How did a major party [Republican] in the world's only superpower," Der Spiegel's U.S. correspondent, Marc Pitzke asked recently, *"become a club of liars, debtors, betrayers,*

adulterers, exaggerators, hypocrites and ignoramuses? These know-nothings are enabled by media outlets neutered by the demands of political correctness. They don't have the guts to say the obvious: These people are daft! Careening to extreme positions that include starting new wars and abandoning old allies (and that's when they even have a position), *they collectively expose a political, economic, geographic, and historical ignorance that makes George W. Bush look like a scholar."*

There's a simple explanation for this bizarre phenomenon. In America's lunatic, gun-toting provincial badlands and rotting urban centers, it's considered suspiciously elitist to show any interest in modern science or the world beyond America's shores. *"Say what you like about British politics,"* Pitzke concluded, *"no European politicians of any party would dare to offer themselves as town dog-catcher while knowing as little about the world as the Republicans."*

The American political system has seldom, if ever, looked as dysfunctional as it does when glimpsed from distant horizons, far-flung worlds. Meanwhile, one thousand American hate groups are growing leaner, meaner, and readying to "take back" a nation they aim to recreate in their own demented image. Heroism without regret, patriotism without scruples, victory without honor.

PRAY TELL, WHO ARE THE MAD?—Yaxkinian children know that the character and evolution of civilizations are determined by the past, and that the past is immutable. So they navigate the present by studying the future. We all possess the gift of retrograde divination: When it comes to augury, nothing foretells the future with greater precision than a history-conscious society. What emerges from the doctrinal struggles that epitomize Earth's travails is a frenzied tug-of-war between conflicting ideas. Essential truths are routinely trampled in the name of doctrine. Earthlings burst with opinions. Much of their mental constructs are erected on a vast scaffolding of dogmas, inferences and pet theories — generally someone else's.

Keen on cramming dormant brain cells, Earthlings adopt simplistic views. They cling to them and claim that they are the offspring of their own cogitations because opinions spare the brain the burden of independent reasoning, because they shield people from what they fear most — inconvenient truths — because make-believe keeps them warm and cozy in their self-spun doctrinal cocoons.

It is impossible to speak of Earthlings in a pre-social state; they exist only in association with others. Sooner or later, association leads to tension, friction, and hostility and, *in extremis,* violence. Generally, Earthlings who are not busy with the stark affair of surviving *[870 million people, or one in eight don't have enough to eat]* fall into two camps: The educated, open-minded, socially-conscious populists *[otherwise known as progressives]* on one side; diehard, blinkered reactionaries *[indulgently self-described as conservatives]* on the other. Both differ in how they perceive reality *[and each other]* and how they propose to influence the human psyche and shape the social order. The former, we have observed, believe that human nature is supple enough so that society can be gradually fine-tuned. The latter think that attempting to improve humankind by retooling nature is senseless. The former believe in free speech and in the right not to believe. The latter put their faith in law, order and some form of creed. And when the two camps gather to do battle over the one institution on which their progeny's future depends — education — they differ sharply on what constitutes useful or proper learning. Progressives advocate curricula that unshackle students from preconceived ideas, syllabi that sharpen the imagination, stimulate inquiry, invite critical thinking, promote social activism and endow future electors with a firm sense of their collective rights in a participatory democracy. Traditionalists demand instruction that instills greater awareness of and devotion to "God" and country.

These dichotomies beg a broader philosophical question, one that we have been struggling to answer for eons: What exactly is an Earthling? In studying this question, and in hopes of avoiding unfair or absurd comparisons with Yaxkin and other mature civilizations, let me simply recount a few salient events and quote from some of Earth's most illustrious thinkers. Their views, recorded from antiquity to recent times, offer a smorgasbord of less-than-flattering self-visualizations. Perhaps some Earthlings will recognize themselves in their blistering observations.

In *Leviathan*, 17th century British self-avowed materialist

Thomas Hobbes says Earthlings are neither good nor bad; he sees them as creatures who crave certain things and who will resort to violence when their desires are in conflict.

> *"If any two men want the same thing, which they cannot practically both possess, they become enemies."*

Writing in *Civil Disobedience*, Henry David Thoreau declared,

> *"There are thousands who are in opinion opposed to slavery and to the war who yet in effect do nothing to put an end to them.... There are nine hundred and ninety-nine patrons of virtue to one virtuous man...."*

The things that Earthlings long for in ways that lead to disputes include material gain, self-preservation, propagation, and an inordinate craving for praise, all of which bring them into a state of tension in which life, in Hobbes's memorable citation, is *"solitary, poor, nasty, brutish, and short."*

For Jean-Jacques Rousseau, the influential 18th century French philosopher, the corruption of Earthlings began with the formation of, and exposure to, organized society. Rousseau sought to find a way of preserving freedom in a world where humans are increasingly *[and grudgingly]* dependent on one another for the satisfaction of their needs. Earthlings are compulsively driven to compete and, when doable, to outdistance and dominate each other. Their one-upmanship, their passion for gain and glory, which to Hobbes was natural, was for Rousseau the result of artificial social conventions that awakened innate neuroses, ignited vile passions and kindled the collective fires of madness:

> *"The first man, who having enclosed a piece of ground, bethought himself of saying, 'this is mine,' and found people*

simple enough to believe him, was the real founder of civil society."

With ownership, which another Frenchman, 19th century social theorist, Pierre Joseph Proudhon, defined as *theft*, came laws, crime, economic instability, social inequality, armies and wars.

Charlie Chaplin, one of the most astute modern social commentators quipped,

> *"Man as an individual is a genius. But men in the mass form a headless monster, a great, brutish idiot that goes where prodded."*

Friedrich Nietzsche, who challenged the foundations of Christianity and traditional morality, noted,

> *"When a hundred men stand together, each of them loses his mind and gets another one."*

Railing against second-hand convictions often modified according to need, Leonardo da Vinci, the prodigy who epitomized the Renaissance humanist ideal, observed,

> *"The greatest deception men suffer is from their own opinions."*

St. Augustine of Hippo, a towering medieval philosopher whose authority and ideas came to exert an enduring influence well into the modern era, advised,

"A thinking being does not make the truth; he finds it,"

Arthur Schopenhauer, among the first philosophers to

suggest that, at its core, the universe is not a rational place, declared,

> *"There is no Absolute, no Reason, no God, no Spirit at work in the world; nothing but the brute, instinctive will to live."*

Baruch Spinoza, one of the most important philosophers *[and certainly the most radical]* of the early modern period whose views inspired strongly democratic political models and who decried the pretensions of Scripture and sectarian religion, wrote,

> *"Scripture ... when it says that God is angry with sinners ... its purpose is not to teach philosophy, nor to render men wise, but to make them obedient."*

Writing in *The Prince*, Niccolo Machiavelli, whose musings have had a widespread and lasting impact, tutored would-be rulers:

> *"Men are so simple, and so much creatures of circumstance, that the deceiver will always find someone ready to be deceived."*

Executed on orders of King Henry VIII, Catholic martyr, Thomas More, who earned a reputation as a leading humanist scholar, railed:

> *"People always talk about the public interest, but all they really care about is themselves and private property."*

Born at a time of religious turmoil and cultural innovation, and one of the most important painters of the Renaissance, Flemish-born Peter Brueghel (The Elder) captioned one of his engravings [*"Everyman"*] with the following observation:

"There is no one who does not seek his own advantage everywhere, no one who does not seek himself in all that he does, no one who does not yearn everywhere for private gain — this one pulls, that one pulls — all have the same love of possessing."

Maimonides, the greatest Jewish philosopher of the medieval period and quite possibly the leading rabbinic authority of all time, author of the *Guide of the Perplexed,* a masterpiece of Jewish thought that seeks to resolve the conflict between religious and secular knowledge, and mocks astrology and superstition, angered both Jews and Christians by proclaiming:

"I call senseless beliefs and degenerate customs diseases of humanity."

Known as the dean of American science-fiction writers, Robert Heinlein counseled:

"Never underestimate the power of human stupidity."

Oscar Wilde, the premier wit and satirist of the Victorian era and the author of rich and dramatic portrayals of the human condition, noted,

"We are all in the gutter, but some of us are looking at the stars."

Deploring the chronic character of human stupidity, fifth century BCE Greek playwright, Aristophanes, remarked,

"You cannot teach a crab to walk straight."

Warning that Earthlings must cease to pursue wealth or else

face catastrophe, Isaiah asked,

> *"Watchman, watchman, what of the night? And the watchman said, 'the morning comes and then the night'."*

Job, an astute critic of his generation, lamented,

> *"They grope in the darkness without light, and He causes them to wander like a drunkard."*

Around the same time, Lao Tzu, a central figure in Chinese culture who advocated humility in leadership and a restrained approach to statecraft, self-effacingly cautioned Earthlings,

> *"If you do not change direction, you risk ending up where you're heading"*

And Albert Camus, who said that the only way to deal with an unfree world, is to become so irrevocably free that one's very existence is an act of rebellion, pithily summed up man's existential dilemma:

> *"Men are not aware of the tremendous energy they must expend just to be normal."*

Two hundred years earlier, Isaac Newton had grumbled,

> *"I can calculate the motion of heavenly bodies but not the madness of people."*

∞

Madness is a non-scientific term referring to mental disorders that are so severe and debilitating as to inhibit licit, socially acceptable comportment. These disorders, rarely observed on other worlds, vary greatly in character and degree. In their mildest form they express themselves as fixations, phobias, eccentricities or exaggerated views of otherwise prosaic events. In more acute cases they can be the matrix from which creative genius or criminality evolves.

There exist on Earth ill-defined forms of mental illness, so subtle, so skillfully concealed and so utterly undetectable that they elude even those trained to recognize the myriad faces behind which they hide. Is he demented who pretends to be sane? Is he who fakes madness—insane? Is conformist behavior proof of sanity? Is a clown "crazy?" Would his antics be sanctioned outside the circus tent? He's only play-acting, you say? What about motorists who willfully exceed the speed limit; are they clear-headed? Are citizens who time after time vote into office inept or corrupt politicians under the ludicrous pretext that they're taking part in the "democratic process"—in full possession of their faculties? Or are they imbeciles who deserve the scoundrels they help elect?

Is the soldier who fires at an enemy he can't see behaving rationally or, to dilute the horror *[or ease his conscience]*, is he pretending to be shooting blanks every time he squeezes the trigger? If not, and should he seek moral justification in sanctioned murder, or derive some secret thrill from it, is he demented, evil or just another wretched victim of military indoctrination? More than a quarter of U.S. soldiers test positive for mental disorders, including depression, panic attacks and Attention Deficit Hyperactivity Disorder *prior* to enlisting; nearly 10% toy with suicide at one time or another. Those who are most at risk of taking their own lives also have a history of impulsive anger, a condition known as "intermittent explosive disorder"—more than five times the rate found in the civilian population. Can one infer from these disturbing statistics that one in four enlistees is driven by psychosis rather than "patriotism..."?

Are boxers who pummel each-other senseless out of their minds? Would their fights-to-the-finish seem less brutish if they didn't appear to enjoy themselves so much? Aren't the fans salivating at the prospect of blood, of a bone-crushing knockout, equally deranged? Does the ball player who scores a goal gain little more than a booster shot of narcissism? Is the losing goalie really forfeiting anything but an inflated ego?"

Are the uninvited missionaries who compel "primitive" peoples to cover their breasts and genitals, who force-feed children alien concepts and rob ancient cultures of their identity, sane or lunatics further unhinged by religious zeal? Is faith in an invisible, unknowable "God" a form of psychosis?

Tune in on Earth's short-wave radio frequencies and listen to the maniacal soul-robbers who lecture their congregants and fill their heads with monstrosities. Look at the transfixed masses of "born-again" who sway and swing and rock, their arms outstretched toward the heavens as they pray for the cleansing firestorms of apocalypse. They believe themselves to be immortal and are filled with love for their neighbors but they are thrown into a state of fury if their divinity is questioned. Are they bonkers or the unwitting casualties of self-induced mass-hysteria?

What about the "prophets" of yore? Were they befuddled talking heads or cunning mischief-makers; clueless prognosticators or schemers blinded by their own morbid fury; soothsayers and mystic diviners who spoke in riddles and esoteric babble or crafty agitators bent on sowing fear in the hearts of men? Were their intentions noble or did they suffer from acute megalomania, monomania, egomania and thanatomania *[Earth's consuming fixation with death]*? Wouldn't these fortunetellers have been diagnosed as certifiably insane, or called charlatans, had modern "psychiatry" not spinelessly declined to see them for what they were—toxic crackpots pickled in gooey mysticism, fanatics prone to treat all inexplicable natural phenomena as the work of an invisible creator? Religious fanaticism is a frequent cause of insanity in Earthlings. Their zeal makes them gloomy and presumptuous; they are easily induced to believe that "God" speaks to them directly and are apt to despise those who do not enjoy such privilege. Didn't the righteous Job tell self-proclaimed seers:

"All of you are quacks!"

Aren't the dream merchants and the healers and the corporate kingpins who deconstruct reality and peddle cheap imitations of Utopia—insufferable psychopaths?

If Earthlings were judged not just for their deeds but for their secret thoughts, their dreams, their hankerings; if they were put away for their natural tendencies *[or for the habits and obsessions they pick up along the way]* dungeons and madhouses would be bursting at the seams. But madness is somehow less reprehensible when it festers in high places; less disgraceful when ruthless tycoons are eulogized for their "initiative," "cunning," and "entrepreneurship;" less ignoble when "my-country-right-or-wrong" flag-wavers brush aside lies, rationalize injustice, defend sleaze and political chicanery; less vile when fanatical proselytizing is hyped as "God's work;" less revolting when illegal and unwinnable wars that enrich bankers and cannon merchants are waged far from home in the name of "national security;" less detestable when freedom of thought is slammed as heresy and when all moral codes are rescinded to protect the interests of the moneyed elite.

Pray tell, who are the mad, and who are the meek who

inherit the wind?

In plumbing their future, it took us no time to realize that what is being demanded of Earthlings are pretense, diffidence, and conformity to a social order more likely to view as "sane" those who surrender their individuality and follow the crowd. To survive, "blend in," average Earthlings must become simpletons stripped of analytical powers and forced to affect a slavish adherence to common expectations of social and emotional "normalcy."

Or else they must fake idiocy lest they be accused of eccentricity.

There's more to madness than meets the eye. Let me count the myriad ways in which I've seen it morph on this mawkishly nicknamed little "blue marble" in the sky where madmen and criminals outnumber creative geniuses a million to one.

THE POOLP & THE GROMOLOK—My fascination with Earth—family and friends have called it "deviant"—is of long duration. It may well have influenced my decision to accept the Alliance's Quixotic mission. I was but a boy when I first read the ancient texts, pored over the fiber-optic discs and eavesdropped on the cacophonous jabbering emitted from Earth by what we still refer to—unkindly perhaps, but not entirely without cause—as semi-rational, unpredictable, babbling bipedal simians. Their origins and evolution are scrupulously recorded in a brief chapter of a bedside volume found in every Yaxkinian home: *The Annals of Biogenic Transmutations and Cosmic Organic Diversity*. Devoted to Earth's earliest hominids, the chapter tells the story of creatures Yaxkinian scribes dubbed the *Poolp* and the *Gromolok*. What the *Annals'* most evocative section, *"On the Rise and Fall of Early Hominid Societies"* reveals, is symptomatic of the eccentricities and iniquities that have for so long plagued Earth and inspired the Alliance's last-ditch efforts to bring this rogue planet to its senses:

"Long, long ago, when time was young and dreams were the measure of all things, there lived on Klipotzk [Earth] beings who rejoiced in their fellows' happiness and grieved their sorrows.

43

We know them as the Poolp[5]. The Poolp were gentle souls given to the arts and noble sciences, poetry, the theater, music, philosophy, and rhetoric.

"The Poolp gathered in sheltered communities, companionable folks drawn together by friendship, the promotion of happiness, and the exercise of a mind free from negative feelings and make-believe.

"As ignorance often fosters strong, generally absurd opinions, the Poolp reasoned that the more uninformed one happens to be, the more opinionated one tends to become. So they avoided linear and rigid reasoning and stuck to facts, simple, observable, irrefutable facts. Whereas opinions are for the most part visceral and unreasoned, and because they lead to vexing oversimplifications or outrageous distortions, the Poolp deduced that advancing views not undergirded by verifiable truths or aimed at spreading knowledge through logic, rational dialogue and cautious speculation was not in the best interest of an enlightened, progressive society. There is no indication, from the artifacts they left behind, that they were in any way prone to mysticism or given to religious rituals. They were as supremely oblivious to the atom as to the existence of an imaginary "Supreme Being."

"The Poolp had an innate grasp of what Earth philosophers and metaphysicians would much later clumsily dub 'determinism' — that every action not only triggers a reaction but that a 'first cause,' and even the failure to initiate a first cause, is the result of a previous causation. They also knew that good deeds invite reciprocal acts of kindness and generosity, whereas indifference or malice engenders rancor and is likely to fuel hostility.

"The context-conscious Poolp had followed a path aimed at securing the fruits of happiness. To them, 'sin' was a misdirected attempt to do a good deed, rather than a premeditated evil act.

---

[5] *The word for "tolerance" in Yaxkinian.* (Translator)

Freedom from pain or distress, they reasoned, is the highest form of pleasure. Such beliefs would much later be defined as Epicureanism; but Epicurus was not yet born when the Poolp chose to live unnoticed, to live the life worth living."

∞

Across a vast and impenetrable forest, on the shores of a lake *The Annals* describe as "the color of pewter," lived a warrior culture that idolized brute force and revered feats of strength, a society in which dying gloriously in battle—even against their own kind—was a source of great pride. They were called the Gromolok, to give them the martial resonance that befitted their temperament: *Grom [muscle]; Olok [being]* or he-man, in our parlance.

"The Gromolok lived in rows of single-occupancy abodes set on cul-de-sacs on either side of well-trodden footpaths. Some flew oversized pennants, others proclaimed their devotion to their favorite spirits — the gods of rivalry and war, of egoism and self-righteousness — with effigies and sacred icons carved of stone and wood. Others yet professed their loyalty to the Khlokh [Code] by warning their neighbors that their domiciles were fortified with all manner of deadly ordnance.

"Unlike the context-oriented Poolp, the Gromolok were rule-driven. 'This is the Khlokh and the Khlokh is absolute,' they chanted. They believed they were speaking on behalf of the 'realm,' a nebulous term they never bothered to explicate. They considered the Code all-encompassing and their system of governance a model to be adopted by all — or else. They had a complicated attitude regarding the world beyond their own, of which they knew close to nothing, and toward which they displayed nervous resentment. They functioned under a kind of three-cornered exceptionalism — the belief that the Khlokh is superior to all other systems; that it must be forced on others, *'for their own good'; and that those who ignore or flout it must be banished from their ranks or worse."*

Isolated and insular as they were, engaged in their own cycle of glory-seeking atrocities, the Gromolok could not tell what was happening across the lake-fronted forest whose pinnacles rose well above their line of sight.

"To the Gromolok—had they only bothered to reconnoiter beyond their sylvan domain—the unpretentious naturalism of the Poolp, their humanism and rejection of supernatural forces would have proved anathema. Spurred by the hazy goal of a 'manifest destiny,' the Gromolok did not care what methods they used to achieve it. At first, they created the myth of their invincibility; then they devised a mechanism by which the myth would be kept alive and exploited. They called it khgrobk ['patriotism']. Long before Ayn Rand rhapsodized selfishness and modern disciples drooled over her vulturine dogmas, egocentric individualism, and hero-worship, the Gromolok saw themselves as epic beings who are beholden to no one but the Code and who are pitted in a life-or-death struggle against imaginary evil forces. Their interpretation of the Khlokh's canons was elastic, self-serving, and decadent. It did not imply self-control and included the belief that all virtues can and must be imposed by force. Hence their glorification of a specialized fighting class, their tendency to regard soldierly might as the supreme ideal of the state, and to subordinate all other interests to the pursuit of war. In short, the Gromolok were double-talking, two-faced hooligans who sacrificed knowledge and refinement for the rewards of power." Support the war fighter.

In contrast, the Poolp had an inborn understanding that unfettered power corrupts the mind, that it blunts the senses and that the ability to empathize with others is sharply abridged. Whereas they knew that power turns people into bullies; that a default brain mechanism causes them to lose compassion when they gain authority over others; that feelings of increased omnipotence shut down [*if the Gromolok ever possessed it*] the mirroring system that enables conscious beings to identify with others, to commiserate — the Gromolok were too dimwitted to fathom, let alone feel, compassion. Once installed, leaders don't recognize themselves in others. Consumed with greed, pride, and an inextinguishable lust for adulation, they are not content to be the masters of their empires; they want to influence their subjects' thoughts and control their actions. Only those who never have to face existential problems preach stoicism to those who cannot avoid them; they don't understand what misery is. Powerful beings are more superficial; their affectations, often the offspring of repressed anxieties, conceal a vindictive streak and can trigger acts of sadism. When individuals appreciate how mutually dependent they are, they realize that empathy and cooperation pay off. But the Gromolok didn't communicate effectively, not even among themselves. They were insensitive, cold, bellicose, borderline paranoid, and despotic — a trait that would harden in their descendants with each passing generation.

The section of *The Annals* that deals with Earth closes with this portentous epilogue:

> *"The Gromolok apparently survived geological upheavals and extreme shifts in climate, but with deforestation and scarce resources exhausted in the aftermath, they turned on each other. Then, one day, they crossed the vast timberland, paddled across the pewter-colored lake on wooden rafts. They raped and*

abducted Poolp women, and exterminated the men and the boys."

∞

Seen in a contemporary context, whether real and forever lost in the mists of cosmic time, or symbolic characters in a morality play penned by ancient fabulists, the Poolp and the Gromolok are the metaphorical stuff that Earth reality is made of. They epitomize the conflicts and sorrows that sunder and, I fear, may ultimately extinguish life on that planet.

THE GROMOLOK SHALL PREVAIL—I remember feeling great sadness when Yaxkin receded from wave motion and I found myself hurtling in Planck time through the blackness of space. I ached for my planet, my family, my friends. And when I reached Earth, I asked myself if I'd bitten more than I could chew.

Earth is not Yaxkin. The ideals we treasure on Yaxkin are nebulous objectives on Earth, not set policies. They exist only on paper and in the hearts of a few principled individuals whose egalitarian views are considered subversive by an uninformed or propagandized mainstream trained to practice self-deception and programmed to reject any view that contradicts its own. At preset cycles, on the eve of formal decision-making sacraments when the mainstream picks its overseers, one is treated to flamboyant speechifying filled with rousing equivocations that produce nary a tangible deed. From what I've observed in the past few Earth-weeks, and after an absence of 50 years, I now seriously question, Earth's ability, indeed its readiness, to meet the rigorous standards for admission to the Alliance.

My misgivings stem in part from the corrupting influence that historical revisionism and the lies that special interests spread to strengthen their control have on the blank canvas of a child's mind. On Earth, history is systematically retooled by biased historians, slanted in the interest of political correctness or religious dogma, and further distorted by opinionated educators or short-sighted parents. Most alarming in an era of instant communications and real-time news broadcasts is what Earth children are *not* taught in school and what truths are routinely redacted, misrepresented or deliberately excluded from curricula and public discourse for fear that they might upset Earthlings' delicate constitutions or ignite their volatile passions.

Yaxkinians are asking: "What do Earthlings tell their children about the unfettered power *[and excesses]* of capitalism, about poverty and hunger, injustice and crumbling infrastructures, about racism and xenophobia, anti-intellectualism and religious fanaticism? What do they say about 'extraordinary renditions;' about the flying machines used to secretly ferry unindicted 'ghost' suspects to a network of clandestine dungeons scattered around the planet where they are routinely tortured; about an agency that skirts the limits of law and morality in pursuit of its missions? How will they explain the long-awaited report *[released in December 2014]* on torture at CIA black sites during the George W. Bush administration which concludes that practices were 'brutal' and ineffective? What rhetorical trickery will they use to justify the severe psychological scarring the detainees endured, the week-long sleep deprivation to which they were subjected, the hallucinations, paranoia, and attempted suicides?" How are my own grandchildren, who'd rather toy with Euclidian, algebraic, and constructive quantum field theory problems—let alone average Yaxkinians and members of our intergalactic community—digest the notion that horrific crimes can legitimately be committed in the name of "national security" and that courts can cover lies or skew laws to favor political elites or commercial interests?

"To survive," my granddaughter Akhlabka remarked recently, "Earthlings would have to reinvent themselves at the molecular level. But *alea iacta est,*" she added. The die is cast.

∞

Akhlabka also observed that Earthlings, who so eagerly kill each other, are full of wrath toward those who try to end their own lives—and fail. Extraordinary efforts are made to revive them so they can be made to die all over again, this time of shame in the court of public opinion. Suicide and euthanasia, rights we honor and vigorously defend on Yaxkin and across our intergalactic community, are regarded as acts of infamy on Earth. And yet, growing numbers of Earthlings are now asking: "Were I racked with pain, stricken with despair, too old and feeble to enjoy life's pleasures, should anyone have the right to deny me the only remedy I have left? Should I be forced to honor conventions enshrined without my consent?"

I have wisely abstained from airing my views on the subject. Earthlings infer from encoded beliefs, not reason. They are programmed to think of life *[theirs—not always others']* as a gift, an indulgence, a "divine" blessing. Any believer looking to rationalize his anger, arrogance, belligerence and bigotry finds validation in Iron Age texts that claim to be authored *[or dictated]* by "God." How obtuse, no, how contemptible a society that decrees that its members must live by diktat rather than conscience? When the "soul" leaves the body, will there be less order, less harmony in the universe? Do Earthlings really believe that their decaying corporeal shell, now transmuted into an ear of corn, a worm, a blade of grass, is less precious to nature; that their immanent essence, now rid of its terrestrial accouterments, is more sublime?

Such notions are born of pride—the foundational sin.

Earthlings do not feel their smallness; they are unconscious of their triviality. They imagine that the demise of a creature as perfect as they will somehow upset the cosmic order.

∞

The purpose of a legal system is to provide an effective substitute for reason in the motives of unreasonable creatures. Rights are nothing without the power that enforces them; therefore might, not right, is the basic tool of Earth's system of governance. This would explain why in certain societies suicide and abortion are considered dastardly offenses, whereas sending youth to their deaths on distant battlefields and snuffing out the life of a felon in an execution chamber are not.

∞

Of course, death is an inconvenience to those who savor the sensation of being. To those who don't, it's a one-way escape hatch. In the best of times, dying is a lonely affair that can be assuaged only by loving those we are fated to leave behind. To be mourned is a bonus we must earn while we're still breathing.

∞

If the "God" of Earthlings is an entity that exists outside their florid imagination, "He" must inevitably be just. If not, he is the most illogical of all concepts. But justice is a human paradigm born of convenience. It is always relative, regardless of who doles it out, whether it is "God," a courtroom judge or an executioner. Yet Earthlings don't always see the connection, but even when they do, they distance themselves from it; they prefer not to look than be blinded by reality; they'd rather risk ignorance than suffer confusion. Human justice raises its voice to stentorian levels but it can hardly be heard over the tumult of human drudgery.

Earthlings commit atrocities when it is in their interest to do so. They are also capable of gratuitous violence. Unlike their primeval and short-lived ancestors, the Poolp, who delighted in the happiness of their peers, modern Earthlings need to indulge their urges, to gratify themselves first. It is the narcissism and arrogance and reptilian intractability of the Gromolok, who exterminated male Poolp and mated with their women, that now flows through their veins. When they invented "God," Earthlings gave it *[human]* traits that are mutually incompatible and cannot possibly exist in the same entity without annulling it. Instead of leaning on reason, vacillating between false hopes and ridiculous fears, they create menacing monsters and seductive specters that alternately terrify them, absolve them of their sins and promise them eternal life in a realm that has no tangible substance or dimension.

There is no such a thing as extemporaneous evil. Evil is not self-created or unrehearsed. It does not evolve in a vacuum. It has a first cause; it is the offspring of necessity or expediency. It was necessity and expediency that incited the Gromolok to pounce on the Poolp, as did Joshua's armies on the Canaanites at Jericho, the Carib on the Arawak, the "Crusaders" on the "heathens," the "Holy Inquisition" on the "heretics," the Conquistadors on the Amerindians, Hitler on the Jews, the Hutu on the Tutsis, the Shia on the Sunni. But is it possible for an omniscient, omnipotent deity to be unjust, cruel and evil? Surely, an all-seeing "God" should epitomize the very essence of righteousness. If the "God" of Earthlings were not just, he would be the cruelest of all beings because his utter lack of interest or involvement in human affairs would have no self-serving purpose. But if such a "God" was real, humans would perforce have to resemble the transcendent spirit that breathed life into them, whom they revere and who, if he really existed, would unavoidably have to be just, compassionate, and loving. Free from the yoke of absurd beliefs, humans too would therefore be fair-minded, rational and upright. But they're not, which would lead one to conclude that their "creator" is as intolerant, irrational and immoral as they are; or else he's just the figment of a troubled imagination sorely lacking a sense of self-worth—which is why they continue to portray this, the most inscrutable human fabrication, as an alternately charitable, comforting, wrathful, tyrannical and mercurial being who grants his finest handiwork the gift of free choice then punishes him for exercising it.

I was thinking about the Poolp and the events that led to their virtual extinction. The more I mingle with Earthlings, the more I am reminded of their precursors' "humaneness," their sense of justice, their spontaneous and undiluted honesty, their instinctive grasp that theirs was a provisional state of being followed by blissful, eternal nonexistence. The Poolp knew suffering and woe but felt them only as a measure of their immense compassion for others. They labored with mutual solicitude and for the common good; they aspired to a tranquil, happy life. They loved their wives, reveled in their tenderness and raised their children to be kind, generous and imaginative. They understood that individual rights must harmonize with collective rights, that justice for all is charity for the self. This may explain why an occasional dominant Poolp gene yields uncommon individuals—poets and artists, novelists and beloved statesmen and holy men who preach wisdom and enlightenment and love, not arcane beliefs.

Sadly, these virtues are being undermined by a rising and headlong freneticism, a time-shrinking haste to experience, possess, exploit, and ultimately destroy what Earthlings deem life's rightful rewards. Call me a cynic: Earth is drifting toward an era of global banditry, with corporate thugs and political racketeers on one side augmenting their ill-gotten fortunes, and packs of roving hoodlums and mercenaries who steal, pillage, and kill to survive the predations that force them into a life of depravity and crime. Wars of the future will first be waged by militias and criminal groups roaming the streets of Earth's largest urban centers. The Gromolok shall have prevailed.

A BRIEF HISTORY OF NIGHT—There was a time on Earth when kings ruled supreme—all great warriors, usurpers, plunderers, and enslavers of men. Some were so powerful [*and so ruthless*] that they convinced their subjects that their power came from "God." Common folk also believed that kings possessed the gift of wizardry, so adept were they at coaxing them to bankroll their wildest undertakings—erecting yet another castle, conscripting destitute peasants to fight their wars, commissioning flattering portraits, marble statuaries and wall-sized tapestries. And the people complied while the kings amassed gold and silver and seized lands to which they had neither divine nor legal right.

∞

Earthlings are made of the same cosmic dust from which we all evolved; and yet they are so gallingly different. Their planet could well be the only corner of the galaxy where violence is systemic, depravity is habitual, and warfare is an irresistible and cyclic pastime.

∞

Past is prologue. To understand Earth's notorious cosmic

egocentricity and fathom its haste to self-immolate, it is useful to look over its shoulder.

During Earth's so-called "Middle Ages," night was neither longer nor shorter than it had ever been but it was infinitely darker, filled with impenetrable shadows, and few ventured into the sulfurous chasm for there, under a thick mantle of ignorance and irrational beliefs, dwelt in untold numbers the loathsome incarnations of man's most hideous fears: Fear of the unknown. Fear of change. Fear of witches, demons, ravenous *incubi,* and insatiable *succubae.* Fear of temptation. Fear of "God's" pitiless tribunal. Fear of Satan and Hades. Fear of sin and eternal damnation.

As day slowly blanched away the blackness, only the sky dared to brighten. The monstrous visions that populated night retreated for a while but they did not vanish. They returned at a time of their own choosing. Day scattered the gloom but it shed no light. It was just an optical illusion, a hesitant and fleeting sensation on the retina, not a higher state of consciousness or wisdom. It was in the full blaze of sunlight that the real horror resumed, this time inflicted on the flesh, not dreamed; branded on the soul, not imagined. The nightmare was real, fed by collective hallucinations that would bloody the pages of Earth's history for the next four centuries and beyond. The plot that drove the story of Earth is one of ceaseless carnage. One can only skim the surface.

In Earth's year 1314, falsely accused of heresy, Jacques de Molay, the last Grand Master of the Knights Templar *[the medieval Church's bankers and hired assassins]* was burned at the stake on orders of Pope Clement V, King Philip IV's sinister *éminence grise.*

"*Maldito*" *[damned, accursed]* is a Spanish epithet reserved at the time for Marranos, the crypto-Jews of the Iberian Peninsula who, by coercion or out of pragmatism born of despair, converted to Christianity in the aftermath of the pogroms of 1391. These *conversos,* as they were also called, numbered more than 100,000. With them the history of the Jews entered a new phase: They were flogged, had their properties seized, were subjected to ruinous taxes, forbidden to trade, often dragged to the baptismal font, and routinely executed.

Hatred of the Jews, fanned 1,000 years earlier by followers of the Jew named Jesus, sparked the onset of the Inquisition in Spain and hastened their mass expulsion.

Marranos were highly cultured, prosperous and influential. Arousing the envy and hostility of the populace, they were hounded and abused by bands of thugs incited by the Catholic clergy. The first in a series of riots against them broke out in Toledo in 1449, leading to pillage and murder. Goaded by two priests, the mob plundered and burned scores of homes. Another attack took place in that city in July 1467. Some 1,600 houses were consumed. Many Marranos perished in the flames or were slain, some by hanging.

Six years later, not to be outdone, the city of Córdoba erupted in a conflict pitting Christians and Marranos. In March 1473, during a religious procession, a young girl carelessly spilled the contents of a chamber pot out her window, splashing an image of the Virgin Mary being paraded on the street below. Hundreds joined in a strident call for revenge. The mob pounced on the Marranos, accusing them of heresy, killing them and burning their houses. Girls were ravaged. Men, women, and children were put to the sword. The massacre and ensuing pillage lasted three days and nights. Surviving Marranos were forcibly expelled from Córdoba. Their houses were ransacked and their possessions purloined. In short, Spanish Jews could not evade anti-Semitic fury by converting.

The advent of the Inquisition was followed by an edict forcing Jews to confinement in their "ghettoes." Issued by King Ferdinand and his wife, [the "Very Catholic"] Queen Isabella, the edict laid the groundwork for the deportation and exile of Spanish Jews. The decree of expulsion materially increased the number, already large, of those who purchased freedom and security in their ancestral homeland — Jews had been living on the Iberian Peninsula for more than five centuries — by submitting to forced baptism.

More obsessive than the Spaniards', the hatred of the Portuguese for the Jews turned to violence in Lisbon. In April 1506, a Dominican priest roused the masses and, crucifix in hand, strutted through the streets of the city, crying "Heresy!" and calling on the people to exterminate the Marranos. More than 500 Marranos were massacred and incinerated on the first day. Young and old, living and dead, were then dragged from their houses and thrown pell-mell upon the pyre. By the second day, at least 2,000 Marranos had perished.

In 1562, foreshadowing *Kristallnacht* and the ensuing genocidal "Final Solution," and to accelerate the planned slaughter of more Marranos, high-ranking Church officials decreed that they be required to wear special insignias. [The yellow star patch would make a comeback four hundred years later, this time, accompanied by identification numbers crudely tattooed on the forearm].

Under constant threat of persecution, destitution and death, Marranos took flight. Thousands emigrated. Some went to Italy, France, Flanders and The Netherlands. Others sailed to the New World. Many trekked to Bulgaria, Greece, Poland, Romania, Russia, and the Levant where, centuries earlier, various tribes had coalesced to found a single nation — the Jews. Others settled as far east as India and China.

∞

Accused by the Church of being a relapsed heretic at a farcical trial engineered to placate the English Court, Joan of Arc was burned at the stake in 1431. Her ashes were dumped in the Seine. Twenty-five years later, a retrial established her innocence and the "Virgin of Orléans" was declared a martyr. It would take nearly 500 years before she was "beatified" *[a status that entitles the faithful to seek the intervention of a dead person in their private affairs. Eleven years later she was canonized a saint and granted a permanent seat in heaven].*

Earthlings have a knack for turning absurdity into sacred art.

HOLY BARBECUES—In 1468 the Flemish city of Ghent was sacked and the first documented Church-mandated tortures and executions were carried out, "to fight the Devil's work."

Alain de la Roche, a French Dominican priest, published an illustrated dissertation on the creatures, some real (toads, snakes, black cats and owls) others wildly fanciful, that "typify sin." The demented tract, an ordained success, was promptly endorsed by the Church and circulated among high-ranking prelates, many of whom no doubt savored some of the work's racy minutiae.

In 1481, acting on behalf of the king and queen, the "Holy Inquisition," under the bestial tutelage of Tomas de Torquemada *[the grandson of a "converso"!]* engaged in wholesale persecution, torture, murder and expropriations masterminded to purge Spain of the Jews and fill the Church's coffers with their impounded possessions.

Six years later, backed by a papal edict, the German inquisitor Heinrich Kramer published the *Malleus Maleficarum*, or Witches' Hammer, a misogynous manual purported to "prove" the existence of witchcraft. Challenging and rebuking skeptics, the *Malleus* claims that witches are more often women who turn their brooms into flying conveyances — than men. It teaches inquisitors how to identify witches and warlocks, describes the physical characteristics of the "possessed" and enumerates the methods *[think "enhanced interrogation techniques" — including water-boarding]* — most effective against a long list of imaginary transgressions, including "casting spells" and "consorting with the devil."

Kramer's handbook was deemed so daft that some clerics condemned it, claiming that it promotes unethical and illegal procedures, and is inconsistent with "Catholic doctrine of demonology...." Then, in the same breath, the clerics wisely conceded that they *"scarcely know why the Lord permits demons to exist, nor how He makes them serve His designs...."*

Even so, repression spiraled and spread like wildfire.

Jews were expelled from Spain. In Portugal they were forced to convert to Christianity — or else. So were the Moors. The persecution continued under the reign of King Philip II and Pope Clement VIII. Openly anti-Semitic, the pontiff associated Jews with usury, the only occupation they were legally entitled to pursue.

Barely concluded, the Hundred Years' War stoked the political and religious discord that cleaved France and England. It would take nearly four centuries for the enmity to abate.

Introduced by seafarers returning from long voyages to the Far East, the plague, cholera and a host of venereal diseases erupted in Western Europe, claiming thousands in their wake. Predictably, the Jews were blamed for spreading these scourges.

Awakened by isolated efforts to breathe fresh air into the Church and challenged by those who aspired to dogmatize it further, religious frictions threatened to destroy the very fabric of Christianity.

Members of a Calvinist sect in Northern Italy were nearly all exterminated by the armies of French king Francis I in a campaign billed as a "crusade against religious perversion."

In 1497, Girolamo Savonarola, the prior of St. Mark's convent in Venice, a book-burner and self-styled moralist, was excommunicated by Pope Alexander VI *[better known as Rodrigo Borgia]*. A year later Savonarola was roasted alive in the public square in Florence where the Bonfire of the Vanities had once blazed. His crime: He preached against narcissism and railed against the clergy's moral turpitude.

Charged with heresy — he had endorsed and promoted the Copernican theory that the Sun, not the Earth, is the center of Earth's solar system — Italian philosopher and pantheist Giordano Bruno was expelled from the Dominican Order in 1576 for arguing something we've known for millennia, that the physical universe is infinite, and asserting that Earthlings are not unique because the presence of life, even that of rational beings, cannot possibly be confined to such an insignificant planet as Earth. Bruno signed his death warrant when he affirmed that absolute knowledge is a myth and that there are no limits to the advancement of learning. He was burned alive in Rome. In Earth's year 2000, on the quadricentennial commemoration of his immolation, the Vatican issued a statement, troubling in its ambiguity and cynicism. It sourly conceded that Bruno's death was *"a sad episode of Christian history"* but insisted that his writings were *"incompatible with Christian thinking and he remains a heretic."*

Earthlings would continue to persecute and murder those among them who see beyond the myopia of their time.

∞

Martin Luther, the firebrand reformer, drove a wedge that irreparably widened the abyss dividing Christians, and altered the course of civilization. His ferocious anti-Semitism, his venomous tracts provided the template for the modern hatred of the Jews. His final vituperations, three days before his death, called for the expulsion of all Jews from Germany.

Heresy is defined as an opinion or system of belief that sharply contrasts with orthodox religious doctrine. Contemporary forms of deviation from "declared" mainstream opinion are variously called "treason," "subversion," "civil disobedience," and "sedition."

In a world swallowed by darkness, not everyone wanted to see the light. Still, it is the very nature of light, however feeble or tentative, to seek an aperture through which it can escape. And even during these murky, cruel times when blind faith smothered sanity and obscured reason, faint streams of clarity emerged and signaled a tardy rebirth, a slow and hesitant cleansing from the madness.

Alive in the uncommon Earthling is the urge and promise of self-knowledge and an intuitive commitment to the rational exploration of the universe around him. This is no easy task, in any epoch, least of all in the Middle Ages when unsupported opinions and unchallenged convictions overshadowed, nay, inhibited, knowledge, when ideological rigidity stifled inquiry and when the human psyche was forever held prisoner by monsters of its own making. It is the desire to free the soul from its shackles and to elevate it to higher spheres of intellect that eventually armed nascent freethinkers with the courage to probe beyond the limits of accepted lore. While new ideas are heresy to the intolerant, they are glimpses of exhilarating and perilous truth to the enlightened who spurn religious authority, resist the tyranny of forced ideas, favor scientific scrutiny and advocate rational discourse. Such profanations of canon law were swiftly and harshly frustrated by the Church. From Saint Peter to recent history, and while proclaiming its "God-given" authority over mere mortals, the papacy exhibited a propensity for greed, corruption, deceit, murder, torture, rape, pedophilia, incest, and prostitution that diverted attention from and weakened the early and hesitant triumphs of tolerance, individualism, and non-conformity.

NATURAL BORN KILLERS—Earth spawned other sorcerers and illusionists, some mightier and nastier than the kings. Gromolok in Poolp's clothing, they were called popes, cardinals, and bishops. Their magic was infinitely more stupefying than any royal sleight-of-hand: They managed to convince the flock that one equals three, that each third is an indivisible whole; that bread is not bread but flesh, that wine is not wine but blood; that pain is good for the soul; and that repentance is the only gateway to eternal life. To keep the faithful in a state of trance-like stupor, popes and princes of the church also decreed that the only knowledge they need to acquire is encapsulated in a single collection of disjointed chronicles that speak of horrific violence, warmongering, incest, treachery, whoredom, and cowardice, interlaced with tall tales, hallucinatory rants, myths, high-handed decrees, absurd taboos, thundering threats, and an occasional elegy.

Popes are the kings of the largest Christian denomination, the Catholics. They are worshipped by millions. Programmed and impassioned, the adulation they command is nothing short of idolatrous. In the past, popes were so redoubtable that even kings feared them: Popes told them who to marry, what country to invade, who to assassinate. They plotted against them, excommunicated them, dethroned them, exiled them, and even had them dispatched to "kingdom come" in the most un-Christian-like manner. Popes engaged in behavior so alien, so abhorrent to Yaxkinian culture that they make our blue skin crawl.

Most Christians never hear a disparaging word about popes, many of whom have risen to mythical status. It's as if a perpetual halo of saintliness hovers over their mitered heads. Yet the history of the papacy bears scant resemblance with reality. Over time, the truth about them has been obscured. Their real persona was so craftily altered or glossed over that few Earthlings realize how decadent and savage most of them were. Egomaniacal, lustful self-promoters who wallowed in vice—traits Catholic historians disguise or suppress—popes were despised and feared by the laity. When the early glow of Enlightenment awakened heretofore rigid minds, freethinkers rebelled against them. Doctrinal disobedience steeled the papacy and led to new pinnacles of barbarism.

With the unctuous gentility of modern papacy as a backdrop, it is hard to imagine that the ancient fathers of Christendom were brutal thugs who retaliated against "heresy" with torture and death. Popes waded through torrents of blood to fulfill their earthly objectives and many led their mercenaries on evangelical fields of battle from which they returned enriched through murder and pillage.

Bishop Liutprand of Cremona, author of the *Antapodosis*, a florid but highly literate satire of the kings of the first half of the 10th century, paints a remarkable if somewhat envious portrait of the debauchery of the popes and their sacerdotal confederates:

"They hunted on horses with gold trappings, feasted at rich banquets with dancing girls when the hunt was over, and retired

> *with these shameless whores to beds lined with silk sheets and gold-embroidered covers. All the Roman bishops were married, and their wives made silk dresses out of the sacred vestments."*

Christian historians dismiss with annoying flippancy the true character of the popes, arguing that they never considered them "faultless." Yet they keep on whitewashing their sordid doings. It is in the nature of proselytism, political or religious, to *mis*-inform when possible, to *dis*-inform when necessary. The truth always drowns in the process.

It all started, like many conquests, with a single proclamation by a self-promoting egomaniac and aimed at simple-minded mortals longing a better morrow:

> *"As he was going along by the Sea of Galilee, He saw Simon Peter and Andrew, the brother of Simon, casting a net in the sea, for they were fishermen. And Jesus said to them, 'Follow me and I will make you become fishers of men.' And they immediately abandoned their nets and followed Him."*

Peter is hailed as the first of twelve disciples. And thus, near the ancient eastern Mediterranean port of Caesarea, according to Matthew's narrative *[written 90 years after the death of Jesus]* and Mark's anonymous and paradoxical account of the same events are uttered the words that launched the Church, made Shimon, hence called Peter, the first pope, and kindled the early fires of anti-Semitism and religious discord.

Thirty-three popes — the first few most certainly Jews — ruled the early "Christian" communities following Jesus's death around 33 C.E. and up until the year 325 C.E. when Christianity was proclaimed an official religion at the Council of Nicaea. In other words, in three centuries, about eight men per Earth-year were elevated to the Church's loftiest rung. *[The turnover rate is said to have been four times higher than that of the busiest whorehouse in Rome]*.

From the beginning, popes established criteria for admittance to Christianity. These norms, which, in defiance of Jesus' alleged ecumenism, excluded "apostates," and other "undesirables," became quickly politicized and incorporated by force into the civil codes of the ruling lay elite. In effect, the state had the power, which it used without scruples, to prosecute and punish what the Church considered crimes against Christianity, thus empowering the clergy and the Catholicized nobility to commit horrific acts of violence.

A papal election was always preceded or followed by shouting matches and fistfights. Careerists and criminals clashed with fanatics and bunglers. What followed were the extravagance, mediocrity, inertia and sleaze, the appalling neutrality and eager connivances, the decadence and the scandals that would sully the Church and give popery the bad name it has never ceased to earn.

Pope Nicholas V (1397-1455) issued a papal bull granting the king of Portugal the right to reduce "Saracens, pagans and other unbelievers" to hereditary slavery, and to kill them if they resist. He is remembered as one of several popes who most clearly endorsed slavery and embodied the Vatican's corruption, sadism, hedonism, and contempt for humanity.

Pope John XII (937-964), one in a long dynasty of dissolute popes, put his mistress Marcia, a prostitute, in charge of his brothel in the Lateran Palace. He *"liked to have around him a collection of Scarlet Women,"* wrote Benedict de Soracte, a 10th century monk-historian the Catholic Encyclopedia smugly disregards. At the pope's trial for the murder of a rival, his clergy swore that he had engaged in incest with his sisters and had raped his nuns. He and his mistresses got so soused at a banquet that they accidentally set fire to the building. In an epoch when the average tenure of a pope was less than two years, John XII sat on St. Peter's throne for a decade. His life came to a sudden and violent end when, according to Church officials, he was slain by the "Devil" while raping a woman. The truth is prosaic and infinitely more gratifying: The "Holy Father" was beaten so severely by the woman's husband that he died of his injuries a week later.

On occasion, the Catholic Encyclopedia provides reluctant accounts of papal misconduct. The scandal surrounding Pope Benedict IX (1012-1056) is a case in point. In 1032, after clawing his way up to the papacy, he promptly excommunicated clerics he considered hostile and launched a reign of terror. He opened the doors of the papal palace to homosexuals and turned it into a lucrative male brothel. His violent and licentious conduct infuriated the citizens of Rome. The Church grudgingly remembers him as

> "... *immoral, cruel and indifferent to spiritual things* ... *depraved and unsuited for the ascetic life. He was the worst pope since John XII."*

Upon his death, undertakers refused to build him a coffin. He was hastily interred in a shroud under the cover of darkness.

According to the testimony of St. Bruno, the learned, and self-effacing founder of the Carthusian Order of cloistered contemplative monks,

> "*The whole Church was in wickedness, holiness had faded, justice had perished, and truth had been buried ... popes and bishops were given to luxury and fornication. They discharged*

their duties, not for Christ but for motives of worldly gain."

Showing contempt for titles, Bruno declined to be made bishop, withdrew with a group of followers and, in 1084, built a monastery at the foot of the French Alps.

Pope Leo IX (1002-1054) was an unscrupulous buccaneer who spent his pontificate sightseeing Europe with a retinue of armed knights and left the world worse than he had found it. The Church calls him "lapsed," coyly admitting that,

> *"He defected from the faith... he fell away by actually offering sacrifice to the false gods."*

Urban II (1042–1099) granted "remission of all sins" to those undertaking "a military enterprise" designed "to liberate eastern churches *[those established in the 'Holy Land']* from heretics" — namely Jews and Muslims.

Callixtus III (1378-1458) banned all interaction between Christians and Jews not calculated to dispossess the Jews. He devoted his reign to turning the major churches of Rome and Europe into torture chambers and satanic temples where daily ritual sacrifices of innocent, men, women, and children took place. People were hung from the rafters to slowly die; they were used as human candles. Cannibalism and depraved sexual acts with victims prior to and after slaughter were rife. The pope fenced stolen property, sold positions of office, indulgences, and sainthoods to the highest bidders, and melted down precious metals for the purpose of funding wars against the "infidels."

Aloof, inaccessible, given to fits of sobbing, utterly inept in statecraft, lacking distinction and achieving nothing of consequence for Italy or Christendom, Paul II (1417-1471) delighted at the sight of naked men being racked and tortured, and displayed an extravagant love of personal splendor that gratified his overblown sense of self-worth. He is remembered as the worst Renaissance pope, a dissolute Earthling who purportedly died of a heart attack while being sodomized by a boy lover. Observing centuries of papal tradition, Paul II maintained a convent full of sex slaves and participated in satanic orgies.

Sixtus IV (1414-1484), a champion of the Spanish Inquisition, sired six illegitimate sons, one the fruit of an incestuous affair with his sister.

Innocent VIII (1432-1492) instigated severe measures against "magicians and witches." He confirmed Torquemada as Grand Inquisitor of Spain. He fabricated fictitious accounts to create a belief in witches, including the claim that witches can fly, change shape and have intercourse with the Devil. Contemptuous of women, whom the Church considered to be destined for little more than fecundity, motherhood, and domesticity, scornful of the institution of marriage, Innocent VIII fathered the largest number of illegitimate children of any pope in the history of the Church. That number is said to be well over one hundred, which is why his reign as Supreme Pontiff would be remembered as the Golden Age of Bastards.

Pius II (1405-1464) wrote and sold pornographic novels while harmless folk were burned alive in satanic rituals across Europe for the slightest peccadillo. He raped his own children and fathered twelve offspring by them. Under his direct orders, individuals were tortured, publicly paraded, and then burned alive in Arras, France, during the Catholic Church's first organized witch-hunts. He showered praise on the Prince of Walachia, the notorious Vlad the Impaler *[Dracul]* who shish-kebab'd his enemies and fickle friends alike.

Known as the Fearsome Pope, Julius II (1443-1513) obtained the pontificate by fraud and bribery.

∞

As night darkens, Leonardo da Vinci is driven underground. No doubt aroused by their sensuality, Pope Paul IV (1476-1559) orders exquisite nudes painted by Michelangelo on the ceiling of the Sistine Chapel to be covered up. Pope Innocent X (1574-1655) has a charming painting by Guercino of Mary breastfeeding a newborn Jesus wrapped in a shirt. Cervantes is placed on the Index Librorum (list of forbidden authors). So are Bacon, Maimonides, Petrarch and Rabelais. Tax-exempt and immune from honest labor, fat and opulent, the Church and the aristocracy harass and exploit sinners and serfs. In their shadow, rich merchants fleece their patrons and bleed the populace.

Across the Atlantic, the plunder of the Americas by bearded, Gromolok-like savages brandishing a sword in one hand and wielding the cross in the other is in full swing, punctuated by forced conversions, looting, rape, and genocide.

Leo X (1475-1521), a homosexual and a shopaholic, financed his spending sprees by selling indulgences, a racket that grants, for a fee, full or partial remission of temporal punishment for sins already forgiven. Under his pontificate, Christianity assumed a refreshingly pagan character. He is said to have uttered, with open contempt for the fraudulent nature of the Gospels:

"How well we know what a profitable superstition this fable of Christ has been for us."

Leo X stands accused of murdering several cardinals who opposed his papacy. He was also responsible for the murder of 70 "witches" following trials involving some 5,000 suspects at Valcamonica, Italy; for the murder of 300 people executed as witches at Como, also in Italy; and for ordering the murder of Aztec emperor Montezuma in Mexico during the *Santa*

Conquista.

Alexander VI (1431-1503), the notorious Mr. Borgia, was without a doubt the most evil and corrupt pope in history. He became a byword for the depraved standards of the papacy. He finagled his way to St. Peter's by ordaining crooked cronies "Princes of the Church" so they could vote for him. He also appointed his son, Cesare, and the teenage brother of one of his mistresses, cardinals. Being the "Holy Father" did not prevent Mr. Borgia from engaging in an active sex life, engineering the murder of his rivals, luxuriating in orgies, and siring seven children. To help "build alliances," he forced his daughter Lucrezia into three miserable unions. Her fourth marriage, to a man she did not dislike, ended in tragedy when the union went sour and the pontiff ordered him stabbed to death. Mr. Borgia encouraged the slave trade in "conquered" lands in the "Indies," to facilitate conversions to Christianity. Some say he died of syphilis.

Paul III (1468-1549) fathered at least three sons and a daughter, and engaged in witchcraft and astrology. He murdered his own mother and niece to secure their inheritance and committed repeated incest upon his children, male and female. He also stands accused of murdering several priests and bishops. He masterminded the founding of the Jesuits. Headed by Iñigo López de Loyola, otherwise known as Saint Ignatius, the order's primary mission was to lead the children of wealthy Europeans away from secularism and enlightenment; instill a doctrine of pseudo-knowledge consistent with Church doctrine; inculcate absolute loyalty to Catholicism; send missionaries and theologians across the globe in search of heresy; assist in conversion; and frustrate the spread of Protestantism. He created the Congregation of the Holy Office of the Inquisition which, twice rechristened, survives to his day. Paul III's rationale:

"Punishment does not take place primarily and per se for the correction and good of the person punished, but for the public good in order that others may become terrified and weaned away from the evils they would commit."

Evil persisted, the terror of religious persecution notwithstanding.

∞

St. Peter Damian (1007-1072), a self-flogging mystic and the fiercest censor of his age, unrolled a frightful picture of decay in clerical morality in the lurid pages of his *Book of Gomorrah*, a curious document that survived centuries of Church cover-ups and book-burnings. He wrote:

"A natural tendency to murder and brutalize appears with the popes. Nor do they have any inclination to conquer their abominable lust; many are seen to have employed into licentiousness for an occasion to the flesh, and hence, using this liberty of theirs, perpetuating every crime."

British historian Lord Acton (1834-1902) summed up the popes' martial nature:

"They not only murdered in the grand style, but they also made murder a legal basis of the Christian Church and a condition of salvation."

Perhaps the popes were dutifully obeying Jesus' command:

"But those mine enemies which would not that I reign over them, bring hither and slay before me." (Luke, 19:27).

Today's Christian clergy works diligently to represent Jesus as an inspired but harmless preacher and a prophet of peace. But they cagily avoid any discussion of a passage from the Gospels that nullifies in one sentence everything Christianity purports to embody. Are proponents of the death penalty and the lunatics who advocate the murder of abortion doctors merely human, or do they knowingly draw their inspiration from that ruthless telltale verse?

∞

The "magnificent" 12th century that the faithful inexplicably glorify above all others of the Dark Ages, began with the Inquisition, which lingered in various forms for the next six centuries, and ushered in the 35-year crusade against the Cathars (also known as the Albigenses). The Catholic Encyclopedia readily acknowledges — and obliquely rationalizes — the Church's arrogance and tyrannical nature when it proclaims that the Inquisition is,

> "...a special ecclesiastical institution for combating or suppressing heresy — 'heresy' meaning 'holding a different opinion'."

Establishment of the Inquisition was the only time in Christian history when the Church was united in purpose and spoke with one voice. The Inquisition became a permanent office of Christianity and, to justify its principles and objectives, the popes introduced a persuasive instrument in the form of fictitious documents known as *The Forged Decretum of Gratian*. The forgeries constitute some of the greatest impostures known to mankind, the most successful and most stubborn in their grip on unenlightened people. In his seminal work, *History of the Conflict Between Religion and*

Science, philosopher John William Draper (1811-1881) calls them,

> *"... a mass of fabrications ... that inculcated that it is lawful to constrain men to goodness, to torture and execute heretics and to confiscate their property; that to kill an excommunicated person is not murder, and that the pope, in his unlimited superiority to all law, is equal with to the Son of God."*

The darker features of that era are not in dispute among honest historians. In this period of Christian history, hundreds of thousands of people were massacred on orders of the Vatican. In 1182, Pope Lucius III grabbed control of the Church and two years later declared the Cathars heretics and mounted a crusade against them. Eighty-six years earlier, in 1096, Pope Urban II approved the first of eight crusades — there would be a total of 19 — and they went on for 475 years. Heresy, the Church declared, was a blow in the face of God and it was the duty of every Christian to kill heretics. Earlier still, Pope Gregory VII publicly asserted that *"the killing of heretics is not murder,"* and decreed it legal for the Church to slay "non-believers." Up until the 19th century, popes forced Christian monarchs to make heresy a crime punishable by death under their civil codes. But it was not heresy that inspired the crusade against the Cathars. Its purpose was to provide the papacy with land and extort additional revenues. The popes engaged in untold brutalities to fulfill these objectives.

The Cathars, a peaceful Christian sect who believed that Earthlings are divine souls trapped in a material world created by an imperfect maker, were now marked by the Catholic hierarchy for extermination. The crusade against them, a demonstration of Church ruthlessness and one of the most appalling massacres in history, began in Béziers, in southern France, on July 22, 1209. What followed was gruesome. During the first few days, more than 6,000 men, women and children were dragged to the Church of St. Mary Magdalene and executed.

Shamefully, condemnation of the Church's horrors against the Cathars, which lasted 45 years *[and during which the small Jewish community in Albi was exterminated]* has been subdued. Worse, there have been serious attempts to downplay the scope of this infamy and devalue the scale of the carnage to irrelevancy. Such efforts to suppress the truth seem to have bolstered the faith of those who wish to believe, against all reality, in the saintliness of the Church. The way mainstream Catholic writers now make light of this dreadful event is unforgivable. The excuse that popes carried out these murders in the name of Christ is indefensible. If Earthlings accept the Church's explanation that Crusaders were brave men who, imbued with deep religious feelings, set out to punish people who veered away from Christ, then they are accepting an untruth. Crusaders were maniacal, blood-thirsty thugs. What is beyond doubt is that as soon as the Catholic armies were mobilized they became the most formidable killing machines Europe had ever known.

And that was just the beginning.

One day, dawn alit and the pestilential haze of ignorance and stubborn attachment to absurd myths slowly began to lift. A pale shaft of nascent self-awareness, a maturing consciousness of the natural world, spread little by little across Western Europe.

As the Intergalactic Security Alliance celebrated yet another anniversary, Gutenberg opened a print shop in

Mainz. A goldsmith by trade, he was the first to use movable-type printing and the originator of the mechanical printing press. His invention fed the fledgling Renaissance and became a major catalyst for the ensuing scientific revolution. Troubled by the spread of heresy *[knowledge]* and always on the lookout for new sources of revenue, a papal court tried to force printers to obtain a license.

The first stock exchange began trading in Antwerp. Copernicus laid the foundations of astronomy and demonstrated the double movement of the planets — rotation about their axes and revolution around their star. A century later, contradicting Biblical assertions (Psalms, Chronicles and Ecclesiastes) which insist that *"the world is firmly established, it cannot be moved,"* Galileo defended Copernicus' heliocentrism. Found "vehemently suspect of heresy" by the Roman Catholic Church, he was ordered imprisoned; the sentence was later commuted to house arrest.

Leonardo da Vinci, architect, painter, sculptor, writer, musician and engineer, painstakingly developed what was at the time the most accurate and comprehensive human anatomical chart. He conceived the screw, the pulley, the articulated wing, the submarine, the helicopter and the armored assault vehicle long before practical uses were found for his ideas.

Concerned not with lofty ideals but with viable governance, the multi-talented Niccolò Machiavelli drew on his own experience and penned his famous satirical treatise on statecraft, *The Prince*. His reputation as a sinister political instigator is unfounded. "Machiavellism," the use of cunning and duplicity in politics, predates *[and follows]* him. Earthlings need no instruction manual to sharpen their natural tendencies.

Alart de Hameel, engraver and architect, supervised the

erection of St. John's cathedral in 's-Hertogenbosch in the province of Brabant in the Low Countries. Lodges of operative masons flourished in the shadow of Europe's great castles and churches. From their workshops speculative Freemasonry would soon emerge.

Erasmus, Dutch humanist, satirist and philosopher, examined the social and religious problems of his day with sobriety and logic. He criticized popular Christian beliefs and infuriated Catholics and Protestants alike. He tried to establish a spiritual commonality on which Catholics and Protestants could agree. His efforts earned him the ire of both camps.

Michelangelo, Rafael, Botticelli, and Dürer created subtle and sophisticated visions that stirred the imagination and awakened dormant or repressed emotions.

Bawdy, irreverent and politically incorrect, Boccaccio, Cervantes and Rabelais turned fantasy, satire and the grotesque into an art form hitherto unequaled in literature.

Less than revered in his own lifetime, Shakespeare, by any other name, will be remembered as the greatest writer in the English language and the world's preeminent dramatist. Transparently anti-royalist and anti-clerical, his sometimes poignant, often scathing, always eloquent portraitures of kings, courtiers, nouveaux riches, simpletons and fools come alive in his plays.

Columbus stumbled upon a New World. His "discovery" forever altered the course of human events.

Antonie van Leeuwenhoek, the "father of microbiology," invented the microscope. The breakthrough, and the findings it educed, put an end to the belief of the time that life is the result of "God"-mandated spontaneous generation. The microscope would later help dispel the notion that diseases are spawned in the "ether" *[the upper regions of Heaven...],* are caused by *"mal aria"* *[bad air]* and are spread by witches and evil spirits.

THE NEW INQUISITION—Holy wars, book burnings, torture, the public execution of "heretics" may no longer be the stock-in-trade of modern papacy, but skullduggery, hypocrisy, and depravity continue to coexist in the marble-clad and gilded realm that professes to guide humans away from evil and into the arms of the "Lord."

As recently as three earth decades ago, Pope John Paul II "the great," a man carelessly hailed a champion of human rights, clashed with supporters of Liberation Theology during his 1983 visit to Central America. In Nicaragua, he publicly chastened the Rev. Ernesto Cardenal, a prominent human rights advocate whom he suspended from the priesthood. He paid a courtesy call on Salvadoran President Armando Calderon Sol, a member of the same political party that engineered the assassination of activist Archbishop Romero and masterminded the massacre of 900 men, women, and children in the village of El Mozote. He then cavorted with barrel-chested colonels and generals instead of kneeling at the graves of six Jesuits slain by U.S.-trained death squads. The Pontiff then "retired" scores of vocal Latin American liberal clerics.

Hastened by papal nepotism strongly biased in favor of diehard bishops, the purge of progressive clergy gained momentum in Latin America. Tragically, in the most Catholic domain on earth, the "Golden Rule" was subverted by hostile attitudes that view the flock at best as unruly sheep, at worst as enemies of the state. Astute and opportunistic, the Church taps into the reactionary power base to maintain both doctrinal monopoly and political custody over the masses.

Like Karl Marx, who despised the proletariat, the Church never fully expiated its disdain of the common people. It steadfastly rejects the notion that Earthlings can govern their conscience without its guidance or control. Worse, it denies them the right to manage their political destinies by delivering them to the same reactionary Pharisaic elite that Jesus is said to have rebuked.

Faced with a choice between Jesus' ethic and political pragmatism, Pope John Paul II sadly opted for the latter. He came to Latin America and told the poor that poverty ennobles the soul. He then urged rich Catholics who bankroll the Church to reject materialism. He might as well have counseled hyenas to give up meat. In casting out the good shepherds of Christianity from the fold, John Paul II also surrendered the herd to the carnivores.

As prefect of the Congregation for the Doctrine of the Faith, John Paul's successor, then pope-in-training, Joseph Cardinal Ratzinger, earned a reputation as a hardline enforcer of Catholic doctrinal absolutism. After heaping syrupy praise on René Descartes, the 17th century French rationalist philosopher *["I think, therefore I am"]*, Ratzinger abruptly withdrew his homage, denounced Descartes and forbade Catholics to read his books "on pain of sin." He condemned Liberation Theology, the oxygen-rich ministry that redefines and, for the poor and voiceless, enlivens the otherwise stolid Roman Catholic pastorate, and he punished its disciples with public humiliations and summary excommunications. He also excoriated and suppressed neo-liberal theologians and delivered hostile orations against abortion, homosexuality, and the ordination of women to the priesthood.

Long since replaced by the plucky archbishop of Buenos Aires, Jorge Mario Bergolio — Pope Francis — and following his baffling resignation, Benedict is still seen as having been insensitive if not hostile towards Jews and Muslims. Critics cite his expanding use of the Tridentine Mass *[which calls for the conversion of Jews to Christianity]* and denounce the reinstatement of four excommunicated bishops, all members of the Society of St. Pius X, a traditionalist and virulently anti-Semitic Catholic organization. One of these bishops, American Richard Williamson, is an outspoken Holocaust denier who struggled to mumble a skewed apology but did not recant his position on the well-documented genocidal event.

Pope Benedict's dealings with Islam — one billion strong and growing at about three percent per year — remained, at best, strained. In 2006 the pontiff delivered a lecture at the University of Regensburg, Germany, where he had served as professor of theology. Titled *"Faith, Reason and the University: Memories and Reflections,"* the lecture was panned by Muslim politicians and religious leaders who protested against what they called "inflammatory rhetoric and an odious mischaracterization of Islam." They were especially offended by the following statement:

> *"Show me just what Muhammad brought that was new and there you will find things only evil and inhuman, such as his command to spread by the sword the faith he preached."*

Benedict never uttered a word about the Crusades, the "Holy Inquisition," or the "Conquista" of the Americas, which, in addition to fattening the Church's bulging coffers, were also waged to spread Christianity ... by the sword.

Other pontifical gaffes would follow, all dramatic evidence of a Church woefully out of touch with reality, to say nothing of how prone it is to tinker with history. On his first visit overseas, Benedict told a gathering of Latin American bishops in Brazil that preaching Jesus and his gospel did not intrude upon or corrupt pre-Columbian cultures. This callous falsehood triggered a storm of indignation, prompting the Vatican to issue a hasty but unconvincing "clarification," not a *mea maxima culpa*. Instead of expressing regret for the evils of colonialism and forced conversions, the clarification indemnified the modern Church by disingenuously claiming that it in no way condones the excesses of the past. *[It just perpetuates them]*.

Distancing himself yet again from actuality, bent on taking the Church back to its darkest days, Benedict, on his first trip to Africa, a continent where at least 25 million people are infected with HIV, told the gathered masses that condoms are not only useless in the prevention of AIDS but that they may actually aggravate the problem. The "cruel epidemic," he orated, should be tackled through "fidelity and abstention." Until the end of his reign, reckless faith or depraved cynicism prevented Benedict from grasping the enormity of his counsel. Pro-life, *[the protoplasmic kind – but indifferent to the dignity of man after birth]* Benedict's outrageous directives condemned millions of Earthlings to an early, agonizing death.

∞

In 1908, the name of the "Holy Inquisition" was changed to *The Sacred Congregation of the Holy Office*. It was again rechristened in 1965 as *The Congregation for the Doctrine of the*

Faith. Cardinal Joseph Alois Ratzinger, the future Pope Benedict XVI, served as Prefect of that all-powerful body whose chief mission is to safeguard and promote Catholic doctrine throughout the world and, in doing so, continues to justify *[or cast a blind eye on]* the unspeakable crimes it committed in its frenetic crusade against heresy. Led by a Byzantine central bureaucracy, the Vatican responds to any deviation from its edicts with swift and wrathful retribution. Adding cynicism to obtuseness, it continues to preach that political necessity is at the root of the Inquisition, past, present and future.

∞

There's more. In 1999, spurning the raw feelings and grievances of world Jewry, Benedict signed an edict proclaiming Pope Pius XII, who reigned from 1939 to 1958, "venerable." The pre-beatification formality was intended to hype the late pontiff's "heroic virtues."

In carrying out the first sacrament leading to canonization, German Pope Benedict no doubt intended to market his predecessor and make him an object of veneration for all Catholics. This initiative was troubling; in so doing, Benedict reopened the long and bitter polemic about the Vatican's attitude toward the Nazis and their ethnocidal objectives. Thus Pius's "heroism" continues to be the subject of heated debate. For 12 years, Eugenio Pacelli, the future Pius XII, served as papal nuncio in Germany. He was then promoted to Vatican Secretary of State in 1933, coinciding with Hitler's rise to power.

Other than a bland Christmas 1942 message that evokes *"people sometimes destined for death or progressive extinction on account of their race,"* Pius XII remained remarkably tight-lipped for the remainder of the war. Since his election in 1939, he had scrapped the encyclical of his predecessor, maverick Pope Pius XI, against capitalism, racism, and anti-Semitism, and deferred to the Nazi state. Worse, he uttered not a word about the "Final Solution," of which he had been aware since 1942. He kept mum about it well after the Reich's last extermination camps were liberated by American, British, and Russian forces. He never protested or condemned the extermination of the Jews whom he viewed, to the end of his days, as the "deicidal race" — Christ killers.

"Sainthood" is a symbolic status. It earns "saints" the reverence of the faithful who, candle in hand, can beg for favors no mortal can grant them. Long dead, they serve no other function than to dwell eternal in the pantheon of Roman Catholicism. But symbolism is a powerful idiom. The enshrinement of Pius XII, in defiance of stirring and widespread objections, speaks volumes about Benedict's own unexpurgated anti-Semitism.

Ex-Pope Benedict is now seen as a man with a record of contestable decisions and regrettable faux pas. Woefully out of touch with reality, oblivious to human nature and disdainful of the secular world, he has reached the ethereal summit of his "profession." The promise of his own beatification in the afterlife has long imparted him with the aloofness of a canonized saint. He is preparing for the final voyage, not with humility and compassion but with the trance-like poise and absent smile of a mystic high on his own godliness. Behind the smile is the seething fury of a wounded reptile. If he can help it, he will not embark for kingdom come without leaving posterity a taste of his own venom: The canonization of a coward.

∞

Popes are no longer feared. They may consider themselves the titular successors of one of the first proto-Christians, the Jewish mystic, Shimon *[dba Peter]*. And it is indeed a rich succession for the treasures they continue to amass and the immense political and economic power they wield, the profligacy, cruelty, debauchery, and un-Christian ways of their forerunners notwithstanding.

And then, there's the money trail. A recent documentary, *Holy Money*, examines the finances of the Holy Roman Church. The pope is not only the shepherd of a billion faithful; he is also the head of a corporate empire of global dimensions that employs millions of people. The Church owns hospitals and universities, gold stocks, and works of art of inestimable value. It attracts donations from all over the world, possesses huge swathes of expensive real estate in the U.S., Italy and in other very surprising places. Today, thanks to a large number of financial crimes, the Church is the richest religious institution on Earth.

Led by University College London Historian John Dickie, the documentary exposes the Church's tortuous relationship with money: from the U.S. where a cardinal allegedly concealed assets to reduce the compensation of victims of child abuse to a religious congregation that traded real estate for political favors; from a monsignor arrested for money laundering to the embezzling of Sunday donations. The "affairs," which involve the highest levels of the Vatican as well as small local parishes, have shaken the confidence of Catholics everywhere.

As *Holy Money* peers into the heart of the Catholic Church's finances it makes abundantly clear that, according to the Bible, *"You can't serve both God and Money."*

"CHIMPANZEES GONE BERSERK"—In a moment of disarming candor, George Edwyn Wolcott, a likable Earthling I recently befriended, and who has better reasons than I to reach the same conclusions about his home planet, exclaimed:

"Let's face it: Humans are just not nice." His is a generic deduction, a one-size-fits-all verdict reached in the sanitized vacuum of upper-crust suburban New England where he lives—not in response to some specific personal affront.

Wolcott is right, of course, but his ruling is tentative, incomplete. Yes, Earthlings can be disagreeable, at times even odious, but some possess seeds of genius that make them somewhat less repulsive. One-third Poolp, two-thirds Gromolok, they are prone to sudden bursts of ferocity, but they are also capable of brief if astonishing acts of valor. They are, as Nietzsche described them, *"all too human,"* and not far on the evolutionary ladder from forebears whose elemental challenge, for millennia, was to survive in a harsh, hostile, often unforgiving environment. Their descendants have since defied gravity, left their footsteps on the "Moon," landed primitive robotic craft on "Mars," sent crude probes on scouting missions to the farthest reaches of the inky void... and pulverized Coventry and Dresden, Le Havre and Rotterdam, Nagasaki and Hiroshima. They produced Socrates and Shakespeare, Leonardo and Locke, Mozart and Michelangelo, Empedocles and Einstein … and spawned Attila and Hitler and Stalin and Mao and Pol Pot and Idi Amin and Ceausescu and Saddam and Kim Il Sung and Pinochet and Gaddafi and ….

Wolcott, a journalist and incurable gadfly who finds no contradiction in these incongruities, challenged his readers in a column published recently by a large metropolitan daily. His closing paragraph read:

> *"I am never more certain of my origins than when I peer into the soulful eyes of a great ape. It's like traveling through time and meeting a long-lost relative. I find comfort and a sense of innocence in this genesis."*

Wolcott, who has an eye for truisms and a flair for irreverence, also likes to tell those most apt to be offended by his jibes that animals possess greater virtues than humans. This is a sentiment shared by many Earthlings but rarely articulated for fear that it might betray an antisocial or blasphemous streak. Wolcott is right; animals can be fierce but they are not "malicious." Malice is deliberate and premeditation is the province of man. A shark is not "mean;" it's a shark. A lamb is not "gentle;" it's a lamb. Earthlings, after learning to dominate their environment—to its detriment—continue to display a calculated taste for savagery that animals lack. Humans are the only creatures that kill for sport. In the end, Earthlings' nobility *[or bestiality]* has never been clearer than in their relationship with animals, who can teach them how to live with grace, love without reserve and, more importantly, how to die with dignity.

Inevitably, repeated before an ever-shrinking circle of friends and acquaintances, Wolcott's epigrammatic witticisms gave some people apoplexy, "lending further credence," as he wrote in a follow-up editorial, "to the notion that blind faith, reinforced by Creationist mantras, will cause otherwise rational beings "to act like chimpanzees gone berserk." Wolcott believes [*as the Poolp did*] that inflexible convictions turn "good" humans bad and "bad" humans worse — a congenital susceptibility for aberrant reasoning and evil notwithstanding.

"We dwell in a spiritual cave age shared by other mentally defective troglodytes," he laments. Who am I to contradict him?

∞

Wolcott rewinds his life and peels the memories like the translucent skin of the Zwibk fruit[6]; it's a pastime that brings tears to his eyes. His interest in history is not purely academic.

"So the Soviet Empire collapsed. U.S. foreign policy, no longer forged in the crucible of Cold War paranoia, is now being crafted to rein in growing foreign nationalism and quell sectarian rebellions ignited by ethnic and religious factionalism and fueled by poverty, corruption, apathy and despair."

Indeed, nascent nationalism is a threat to no one but a few corporations that mine and smelt metals, extract and refine non-renewable fuels from the bowels of Earth, pollute the air, poison oceans, lakes, and rivers, raze forests, control the media, bribe lawmakers, set wages, murder union organizers, export their earnings and enrich their stockholders by sucking dry the economic marrow of poor nations, then shutting down their operations and leaving large swatches of land

---

[6] *Onion* (?) (Translator)

scarred, toxic, and useless.

∞

One can be a patriot and a scoundrel. Nationalism and villainy are not mutually exclusive. Earth is now facing a truth emergency so dire that states lie, commit fraud, and employ anti-terrorism measures, spy networks, mass imprisonment, torture, slavery, and assassination to suppress it. Much of what is happening can be laid at the public policy doorstep of a small number of super-nations that continue to trade integrity and justice for hegemonic power and economic dominance. The peoples of Earth are beginning to realize that their governments' primary mission is to protect the wealthy and to insure capital expansion worldwide. The U.S. military, which spends more than any other nation, is the brain, nerve, and muscle behind a global protect-capital-at-all-costs agenda. For now, the U.S. and European Union members are vigorously forging increasingly destructive regional and bilateral agreements that extract enormous and irreversible concessions from developing countries, while offering close to nothing in return.

Meanwhile, in Central America, Wolcott's old stomping grounds, the human rights picture grows dimmer even after years of torpid peace and an era of coerced "appeasement" during which U.S.-trained military thugs were pardoned and the dead were forgotten. Prospects for change yielded little or nothing. No viable political opposition has yet emerged. Instead, dynastic despots succeeded one another. Impunity reigns. Kidnappers, torturers, and assassins bribe their way out of jail. Generals and colonels implicated in human rights abuses *[sanctioned by the U.S.]* are acquitted and absolved in the name of "national reconciliation," whereas their victims and their families are trivialized and ignored.

Poverty festers as markets based on coffee, sugar, bananas, and foreign-owned sweatshops fail to compete in the global economy. Heads of state are incapable or unwilling to deal with soaring delinquency and violence. They respond instead with woefully ineffectual "zero tolerance" policies that trigger orgies of social cleansing. "Undesirables" are liquidated, among them homeless children.

It's a mess and Wolcott scrupulously reports what he sees. He likens the situation to a succession of cease-fires rather than a permanent end to hostilities because the problems that trigger uprisings and wars are still in place — ham-fisted and corruptible plutocrats and a depraved eagerness by the world's banker/self-appointed enforcer, the U.S., to coddle them so long as they vow to keep a fictional "red menace" at bay. He argues, in vain, that governments must reflect the aspirations of the people they rule only to concede that the people are ungovernable. Apathy is the sedative of the masses, he laments. It prevents them from grasping the precariousness, the irrelevance of their lives.

High-born, Wolcott suffers from a common and spreading Earthly disorder: He inhabits his past the way Diogenes occupied his barrel — a loner given to periodic fits of acrimony and despair. Whereas Diogenes sought to acquire "Further Light" *[knowledge]* in the shadowy regions of human credulity, malice and stupidity, my human friend retreats into the darkness of his own ruminations. Spurning logic, given to self-treachery, he insists that yesterday was wholesome and joyful. He dreads the present. He lives in fear of tomorrow. A casualty of his own selective memory, he is visited, he tells me, by black-and-white recollections of a "Gatsby-like" adolescence, of doting parents and foppish peers stylishly attired in the latest art deco couture. He dredges up silver-screen memories of cruises to exotic locales, winters in Zermatt, lavish suppers at La Tour d'Argent in Paris, gala performances at London's Covent Garden and lazy afternoon tennis parties spent sipping Veuve Cliquot in fluted crystal glasses at his parents' Greenwich estate. He replays halcyon days filled with improbable metaphors further dulled by the passage of time. He stopped wearing a watch for fear that each ticking second pulls him nearer to the brink.

In his armoire hangs the elegant ensemble in which he will be buried—a black velvet Dior suit, a pink poplin shirt and Italian silk vintage necktie bought in Milan for the occasion twenty years ago. He fears death but, damn it, he will put himself on display in a satin-lined open casket, suitably made up, a hint of rouge adorning his lips, a white carnation pinned to his lapel. He cares not a whit about today but he will take his final curtain call with studied chic as his life fades into sepia-tone images of a time and place now awash in indelible grayness.

"I don't understand you," I tell him.

"How could you? You're not of this world."

"You have a point," I concede. "But, surely, there are norms even on Earth."

"What can I say, that's who I am," Wolcott snaps back.

"That's who you engineered," I retort.

"I'm too old to change." There is weariness in his voice.

"No. You resist change."

The humble reed sways and bends and surrenders to the wind. The mighty oak tenses up, stiffens, snaps like a twig and topples over. Everyone can change. I feel sorry for Wolcott but I must not preach the Yaxkinian virtues of positive thinking, will power, and optimism. His is the symptom of a growing malady on Earth: Paralyzing pessimism in the face of reality by some, a longing for reactionary values and faith-based strictures by others.

We, Yaxkinians, live on the cusp of a never-ending tomorrow. Millennia of introspection, learning, and prescience taught us not to dawdle in the past but to keep an eagle eye on the future. The past is gone. It can't be altered, revived or updated. We revisit it on occasion when memory beckons, or in the service of history. The sojourn is brief and utterly lacking the tinges of maudlin melancholy that color my human friend's reminiscences.

Wolcott is mired in the rose water-scented dreams where yesterday's evanescent specters congregate. I find his narcissistic fixation on "olden times" a noxious fad and a colossal waste of time. The past is irreversible, I tell him. He should file it away in the dark and dusty attic where he keeps bric-a-brac and boxfuls of hand-written letters and yellowed photographs. But for Wolcott, yesterday is a refuge and a prison. He has committed himself there until the end of time. His beloved grandmother's assertions that her world was as decadent and cruel as his had no effect on him. Unlike us, he has no memory of the future.

The surest way to let the past intrude is to relive it. There is a sadomasochistic component to Wolcott's obsession with death that prevents him from navigating the present and charting what comes next. Lurking under his morbid fixation is a large dose of narcissism. Some Earthlings enjoy marinating in their own noxious juices; it gives them a deceptive if caustic sense of selfhood.

∞

"Even as a child I'd rather read, listen to the radio, and daydream. My parents would urge me to go out and play but I had few friends, at least none with whom I shared any degree of intimacy. I was never a 'party' person. On those rare occasions when I accepted an invitation, I could be found leaning against a wall at the far end of the room, surveying the incomprehensible merriment around me and asking myself, 'What the fuck am I doing here?'."

Not everyone is suited for an eremitic existence. It takes the kind of misanthropy that comes with experience to shut the door on the world. Looking back, Wolcott thinks he was born a recluse. It's an allegation made to justify what he's become, not what he was.

So here I am here on Earth. I will spend the next few lunar phases in earnest but pointless exertions. I can't wait to return to Yaxkin, to rejoin my family and friends, to reconnect with my inner self, to surrender to life's alluring embrace. More useful than the past, more predictable than the future, is an existential realm that is tangible and lucid, at once fleeting and ceaseless. It's the *now,* a place not bounded by geometry, a circumstance unmarked by clocks. For those who have the courage to settle in its ineffable actuality, it's the only place to be. Anyone yearning to break free from the shackles of the past and the ambiguities of the future will always find a warm welcome in its bosom.

I didn't have to cross such galactic distances to apprehend the obvious. But serendipity is where you find it. When I return to Yaxkin, cleansed and brimming with a thousand spare tomorrows, I will think of Wolcott and others like him who, submerged under the weight of a thousand yesterdays, can find no peace. Because they have ceased to dream, they have also ceased to be.

MY MOSCOW NIGHTS—It may seem presumptuous for a stranger, an "alien," to pass judgment on the human race, to deconstruct that most perplexing of all creatures—Earthlings. I spent a decade observing them up close. Prone as they are to act first and think later, trying to plumb their psyche, to explicate their naïveté and delusions, is never easy, nor always safe.

∞

I remember Moscow. Strolling along the wooded lanes of Krasnopresnensky Park, near the banks of the Moskva River, I saw lovers kissing as they do everywhere when spring alights and lust, like sap, percolates through the veins and flushes out winter's numbing grip. Pigeons cooed, pecking at the graveled walkways, migrating geese waddled to and fro in search of a crumb or two. Sparrows chirped boisterously in a tongue understood by sparrows from Central Park and the Tuileries Gardens to the Great Wall of China. Overdressed red-cheeked toddlers frolicked under the half-attentive gaze of stern-faced parents. Huddled on a bench barely wide enough for three, five furrowed matriarchs, their heads covered with kerchiefs, knitted furiously in unison as if driven by some invisible taskmaster.

From a small humpbacked bridge, her reflection playing brightly in the pond below, a little girl with a huge white bow in her flaxen hair cast a baitless hook in the fishless water. Poised for a strike that could never be, her eyes fixed on the concentric circles radiating away from the quivering line, she waited. I recorded her likeness from a distance. She may still be there for all I know, undaunted, Quixotically defiant, a symbol of the Russian quest for the impossible dream.

Nearly a century after the October Revolution, I thought as I gazed at that beautiful child, dreams are especially useful. They help deflect an existence colored by yesterday's nightmares and corrupted by a national psyche that would rather bring back the Bolshevik straightjacket than savor the risks and rewards of free will. Dreams, when carefully managed, suspend reality or, at worst, blunt it for a while. What cannot be prevented must be endured.

Gray and gritty, dusk slowly settled on Moscow like a shroud, accentuating the surreal flamboyance of the Ukraina Hotel rising in the distance across the river's murky waters. Dusk would linger for an hour or so, swallowing shadows and jealously postponing night which, like all my Moscow nights, would be spent awaiting dawn. Krasnopresnensky Park was now nearly deserted; bands of young drunken ruffians, I knew, would soon be on the prowl.

I returned to my room at the Mezhdunarodnaya Hotel, past the unavoidable "floor lady," a KGB matron of redoubtable girth endowed with a persistent stare and an inquisitorial manner. I bolted the door behind me, more out of symbolism than pragmatism, and settled down to 30 minutes of news on CNN, at the time the only lucid window on the outside world.

Following the news, another slice of the Soviet dream was being dished out for all to feast on, like manna from heaven. Dr. Anatoli Kashpirovsky, the alchemical man, miracle maker, psychic healer extraordinaire, and perestroika prophet, was about to bend the airwaves, as Uri Geller would a spoon.

In lifting countless taboos, perestroika, or "restructuring," reopened the floodgates of credulity among a people noted for their mysticism. Sensing a craving for miracles, fortified by mounting social and economic problems, Kashpirovsky had galvanized the Russian people, many of whom, haunted by apocalyptic visions, were willing to entrust their fate to telepathic sleights of hand for the grandest dream of all—a cure against despair. This time, perestroika had aimed at far more than meets the eye, the blunted eye, that is, of television viewers who, night after night, were being lulled into insensitivity by the ubiquitous drone of political speechmaking. It may in fact have sought to conquer the wounded Slavic soul by seducing its weary optic nerve.

Such seems to have inspired the launching of a fortnightly prime-time program promising relief against everything from acne to senility, gout to cancer and, the architects of perestroika hoped, would shake off the inertia and emotional paralysis of post-Soviet Russia.

It failed on all counts.

While reformers had quickly understood that social and political changes can help reduce the de-civilizing effects of past repression, no restructuring, however swift and radical, can eliminate them all. Ultimately, the individual must come to terms with society by adjusting to it. Television, the reformers thought, could act as a therapeutic go-between and kick-start a re-humanization process.

Positioned to follow the Sunday evening news broadcast, "Time," a mild anesthetic in the bountiful pharmacopoeia of Russian TV soporifics, the program reached two hundred million viewers, all of whom anxiously focused their wistful pupils and battered psyches on the soulful eyes of the charismatic hypnotist and healer, Dr. Anatoly Kashpirovsky.

The rationale was deceptively simple. "There are too many sick people in this country," Kashpirovsky had told network executives. "I will talk to them, touch them. I will reshape their egos as I entertain them. What have we got to lose? Our healthcare care system is so archaic."

This was an understatement. Hospitals were shorthanded, overcrowded. Their dank hallways, where the sick and the bloodied waited to be doctored, smelled of sweat, urine, putrefying viscera, and excrement. More than two-thirds of Russia's 4,000 rural hospitals lacked hot water and more than one-third had no sewers or indoor plumbing. Despite a thriving black market, pharmaceuticals were scarce.

But the crisis had reached the cities as well. A paucity of modern surgical equipment, including disposable hypodermic syringes and needles, inadequate post-operative facilities and an acute shortage of nurses and technicians had forced the National Institute of Orthopedic Medicine to limit the number of operations it could perform to five or six a year.

"It may take our physicians five hundred years to reach all of the sick and infirm," Kashpirovsky had melodramatically warned. "Only the unshakable belief in a wondrous and heretofore untested oracle can help. I have an antidote against all human ills and it's as easy to administer as turning on the TV.

"Think of it as mass-market medicine," Kashpirovsky had added. "Millions of people can seek and be granted a miracle in the privacy of their own home just by peering into their television screens. And it's free!"

In only a few weeks, Kashpirovsky had insisted, devastating illnesses, some in their terminal stages, could be reversed or cured. Tumors, cerebral lesions would shrink and disappear. The blind would see again. Warts, scars, migraines, insomnia—"a mere trifle" for Kashpirovsky—would vanish.

The bald were promised full heads of hair; the impotent, the libido of a Siberian tiger.

Delivered against a bland musical backdrop, Kashpirovsky's pronouncements were designed to conquer incredulity, neutralize cynicism, and overcome doubt. "Whether you're watching me or going about your household chores," he intoned with rapt eloquence, "you're now under my spell. You're healing yourselves. Faith in the mystery of miracles," Kashpirovsky preached smugly, "augments my curative powers." He was the shepherd who pardons an errant flock, the savior who absolves the unbelievers who denigrate him, the redeemer who exonerates the pitiable skeptics who scoff.

The program had none of the tawdry glitter of American televangelism. Absent were the sumptuous stage settings, the cosmic lighting displays, the ethereal vaulted spaces that seem to reach out to heaven and from which are echoed the stentorian voices of the pastors. Such stratagems do not work on the mystical Russian soul. Instead, Soviet-gray, proletarian-drab reality in its most elemental manifestation helped deepen the urgency of salvation.

His eyes lost in an all-knowing void, exuding serenity and boundless love, Kashpirovsky managed to reduce audiences to cataleptic trances and other states of exaltation resembling extreme religious fervor. That would prove to be his undoing.

On the eve of the 11th Congress of the People's Deputies, the Soviets had suddenly been offered a double ration of television therapy: Hypnosis on Saturday, to mend the soul; a political sermon on Sunday, to reshape perceptions, reform behavior. Who knows, the architects of perestroika had reasoned, perhaps faith in miracle-laced propaganda can help us too. Their benevolence—or their gullibility—was short-lived. Whereas writers continued to mix metaphors on Sundays in the name of social equilibrium, Kashpirovsky, show-biz demi-god and prime-time exorcist, was suddenly taken off the air. In the rich lexicon of Soviet euphemisms, his brand of "healing" was deemed "counterproductive." It may have been more than even perestroika could bargain for. Not unlike Mephisto, Kashpirovsky had bartered the souls of his flock against the promise of an afterlife as a TV celebrity.

Born of an ideological crisis, incapable of dusting off the unraveling webs of "communism" and thus depriving itself of the comforts of a hereafter, perestroika failed to ensure liberty, to kindle abundance, to hasten the end of economic exploitation, to inspire and bring about social equilibrium. The new Russian classes faced an awesome problem: Miracles like hot running water or uninterrupted telephone service or fully stocked grocery shelves would continue to be transient phenomena. After all, too much of a good thing can corrupt the masses. And many will wonder, as the nightmare lingers on, what schism can the malcontent turn to, what shape will idealism and humanism and justice take now that "communism" is dead?

∞

Members of the Intergalactic Security Alliance regard capitalism as a system that sacrifices the masses at the altar of personal profit. We call it a "form of economic cannibalism." Instead of limiting the entitlements of the rich, unfettered capitalism continues to strangle the poor by slashing or abolishing the social programs that keep them barely one step away from homelessness and starvation. The rate of capital return in developed countries has been persistently greater than the rate of economic growth, thus causing wealth inequality to increase. Tax "adjustments," deferrals and cuts for the rich have reduced their financial obligations to society. This trend has led to the rise of what French economist

Thomas Picketty calls "patrimonial capitalism," in which a few families control most of the wealth. Inequality is not an accident but rather a feature of capitalism that can be reversed only through a progressive global tax on wealth. Piketty challenges the assumption that free markets automatically deliver widespread prosperity. Instead, he warns, the rich will get richer, and everyone else will find it nearly impossible to catch up. Unless capitalism is reformed, the very democratic order will be upended.

This position does not prevent us from viewing "communism" — as it has so far been practiced — as a doctrine that recruits the maladjusted and the malcontent and sacrifices them at the altar of the Party.

It is because the term fails to convey the concepts it purports to encapsulate that we put "communism" in quotation marks and read it thus circumscribed in the works of others, as if to accentuate an incongruity. The word is a paragon of vagueness. Overuse, misuse, and abuse do that to words. "Progressives," "loyalists," "conservatives," "liberals," and "independents" know what I mean. It's not surprising that Marxists, atheists, human rights crusaders, freethinkers, pacifists, and people who wear red socks have all been at one time or another labeled "communists." In McCarthyist America, artistic non-conformity and a penchant for social justice were unmistakable symptoms of "communism." Social activism is still looked on askance by right-wing demagogues. Popular liberation movements aiming to shake the colonial yoke are similarly imputed. Opposition to U.S. military intervention in such conflicts, when not spurred by laissez-faire isolationism, is also denounced as "communist-inspired." John Lennon's stirring pleas for peace at a time of war were reflexively ascribed to "communist leanings." Had they lived today, Thomas Paine and Henry David Thoreau would also be branded left-wing radicals. And Jesus would be re-crucified for preaching social justice.

There's another problem. What passes as "communism" is a perversion of the ideals it alleges to represent. It has also betrayed the goals to which it is theoretically committed. In assuming power by force, self-styled "communists" — hooligans and profiteers — granted themselves rights that they promptly took away from the rank and file. Instead of tending to urgent social issues, such as poverty, hunger, and illiteracy, their crusade quickly became mired in proselytism-by-terror.

Ultimately, the narrow canons at the core of "communism's" wider philosophical tenets, like those of monotheistic religions, are simply unenforceable. Driven by disciplines and proscriptions that denounce egotism, intolerance, and greed — traits found in abundance in Earthlings and indispensable to the preservation of the self *[and the perpetuation of capitalism]* — real "communism" is hopelessly incompatible with human nature. What the world has witnessed since Marxist theories were first propounded is a travesty wrapped in parody. Under the brutal stewardship of its fascist disciples, "communism" has failed. History may yet rank this fiasco *[as is religion's inability to root out evil]* as one of the greatest tragedies to befall the family of man. Had Marxism been given a chance, Earthlings would be at peace instead of being captive to the capitalistic politics of austerity and environmental degradation that impoverish children, gut social safety nets, and threaten the planet's future.

Meanwhile, Russia's economy is teetering on the brink of recession. Inflation is on the rise. The ruble has lost 30% of its value. Small businesses are closing shop. And Dr. Anatoly Kashpirovsky has since been elected a deputy of the Russian lower house and has returned to mass healing. Oh, how Earthlings favor deception over reality.

THE TERRITORIAL IMPERATIVE—Cities are Earth's souls revealed. On their streets, in their Babel-like architectural creations, in the pulse, speed and resonance of pedestrian and vehicular traffic, in their arts centers and teeming eateries can be glimpsed the feverish pace that animates them, endows them with individuality and, to their credit, epitomizes Earthlings' embryonic, disorderly, and raucous intellect.

City dwellers are amazingly resourceful and surprisingly adaptable. They have to be to endure the somatic stresses and emotional ordeals to which they are repeatedly subjected. As a result, they have developed phenomenal survival strategies and learned to exploit a rich array of inborn and acquired traits, all designed to protect or augment their colossal egos. Tolerable as they can be individually and in homeopathic doses—traces of Poolp ancestry occasionally emerge—it is when they assemble for work or play that the dominant Gromolok self-image, fierce territoriality, and cutthroat rivalry boil over like magma from a colicky volcano.

There is in the human animal a relentless compulsion to ensure that he will not go unnoticed, ignored, or disparaged. The higher the status achieved by an individual in an organized setting, the greater the amount of time he devotes to ego-preening activities. Generally, the more preoccupied they are with the demands of ego-maintenance, the more readily Earthlings flout the duties they are being paid to perform. It is also characteristic of Earthlings employed in hierarchical settings to opine that those of higher rank, or occupying statelier positions than they, are actually quite unfit for the job. Humans are especially loath to serve or be ruled by their equals, less yet by those they consider intellectually or functionally inferior.

Some of the most inept *[but ego-bursting]* Earthlings can often be found in positions of political authority—collectively called "civil service" or "government"—in which incompetence increases in proportion to rank and stature, and whose labors are unrelated, sometimes even inimical to the concerns and aspirations of those they have been elected or appointed to represent, serve, and protect.

Regardless of the positions they occupy, government workers are commonly insecure individuals who are programmed to work at the highest acceptable level of incompetence. To justify their existence, some invent great quantities of essentially meaningless work. Others defend their delicate egos by surrendering to intoxicants—depressants or stimulants—that diminish their productivity even further but never seem to compromise their position because, to a certain extent and at varying intervals, their superiors, equals, and subordinates also seek relief from mind-numbing chores by indulging in mood-altering substances.

Everything about the human animal is tied to territoriality. Oftentimes, "bureaucrats" join forces and erect clandestine ego pantheons that can be managed and defended only as a group endeavor. These conspiratorial alliances are called "cliques." Maintaining control against competing coteries is essential as it protects them from prying eyes while lending them an air of false importance. Cliques often unwittingly work on the same assignments — with comparable lack of skill and identical results.

Not everyone is able, or eager, to work in a group. Many Earthlings, I've observed, would rather shield their ego by staying in the wings, a place where they can inflate themselves all out of proportion to their professional worth and the magnitude of the tasks they're called to accomplish. Such individuals are rarely found at the summit of an organizational pyramid. Despite their bombast and posturing, they are quite insignificant. All too often, especially in government settings, insignificant people are elevated to positions of eminence and power. Temperamentally insecure, their self-esteem now on the line, taking themselves more seriously than they deserve, they instantly mutate into pokerfaced, arrogant and double-crossing despots who hide behind closed doors, doing close to nothing, but secure in the knowledge that being unavailable makes them appear quite indispensable. When aloofness and pomposity fail to confer the distinction they crave, they mend their delicate egos by sullying everyone else around them. Making others look bad is an efficient psychological ploy that works best at the lowest rungs of officialdom. A confrontational attitude is often the best defense against accusations of ineptitude, sloth and venality. In government, where sclerotic incompetence and primping self-promotion are so pervasive as to render the whole system untrustworthy, conceit and bitchiness are a pathway to awards, promotions, hefty raises, and generous year-end bonuses.

Found in mid-level management positions are some of the most exotic bureaucrats. They have been compared to fitness buffs who exercise on silly contraptions Earthlings call "treadmills." Huffing and puffing, they walk or sprint and expend great thermodynamic capital, but the scenery around them never seems to change; they never get anywhere. These pen-pushers defend their exertions as evidence of their diligence *[or patriotism]*. They are, in fact, utterly useless but they rarely lose their jobs as the bosses who hire them—and to whom they are beholden—also run in place and are just as incompetent.

Overseers, I've noted, take management courses reminiscent of the method-acting techniques that thespians use to create in themselves the mindset and emotions of the characters they are to incarnate. To give lifelike performances, "supervisors" avoid ego involvement with their peers and underlings by faking serene indifference for everything that happens around them. Their facial expressions convey studied concern for the myriad responsibilities that dog them; they look deep in thought, whereas they really don't give a damn about anything or anyone except the bureaucratic protocols and loopholes that favor their continued employment. They never miss an opportunity to underscore their own importance. Their craggy brows and sullen expressions mask a secret exultation: They are assisted by loyal flunkies who do the grunt work and take the fall on their behalf; and they earn indecent salaries that will increase in proportion to their appalling mediocrity.

WHAT THE SELF PERCEIVES—Separated by interstellar space-time, Earth physicist Albert Einstein and Ahauk Bkuluxk, Yaxkin's poet laureate, distinguished professor of ethics and chairman of the Intergalactic Security Alliance, both pondered relativity—the former to postulate radical if incomplete cosmic laws, the latter to explore the metaphysical realm. Both reached broadly similar conclusions, among them that perception depends on vantage point.

Bkuluxk supported his argument by quoting from a disquieting if prophetic story that every Yaxkinian schoolchild is taught to ponder: Visitors from a faraway planet land on Earth for the first time. They are taken to a magnificent palace. Ushered into the king's [or Pope's] chambers, they notice Earthlings bowing and kneeling before him. Some genuflect and place their foreheads upon his jewel-encrusted robes. Others kiss his feet. Awestruck, the space travelers conclude that their host must be a great and saintly man, or else why would his entourage engage in such displays of sycophancy?

The visitors are then transported to a coal mine. There they see spectral beings with blackened faces hunched over the unyielding rock, toiling from dawn to twilight in the bowels of Earth in suffocating near-darkness. Surely these Earthlings must be unrepentant evil-doers, the extraterrestrials reason, or else they would have been spared such wretched existence.

Much of human consciousness is based, not on fact, Bkuluxk teaches, but on how Earthlings are conditioned to interpret the occurrence of living. There are no wrong answers, only divergent viewpoints, which are themselves blurred by conformity to a particular optic. Truth is in the mind's eye of the beholder. Bkuluxk went a step further. He put forward that perceptions can actually alter the experience of reality. I had an opportunity to test this strange concept, not in the seamless geometry of space, nor in the sterile labyrinths of Cartesian logic, but in two equally dissimilar yet contiguous regions of the human condition. I went to Central America to see for myself what George Edwyn Wolcott had assured me would be the extreme manifestation of an alternate reality and a life-changing experience.

I attended a reception at a posh hotel in Guatemala City. I crossed paths with corpulent, bejeweled women, most of them painted to camouflage the ravages of time. I shook hands with sweet-smelling, self-important burly men in elegant double-breasted suits, silk ties, and snake-skin shoes. I engaged in small talk and endured the syrupy babble between those who came to be seen and those who insist on being heard. Wealth, influence, power, all vied for attention as fragrant wines and succulent finger foods traveled on silver trays carted by white-gloved mestizo lackeys. Such ostentation, I mused, must be evidence of great virtue, the well-earned entitlements of the righteous, the uncorrupted, the "God-blessed."

Early the next morning, on my way to another high-level parley downtown where the uncorrupted never venture, I came upon sleepy-eyed, malnourished children pulling heavy loads, sweaty campesinos packed like sardines in rickety smoke-belching trucks, half submerged under the provisions they bring to market from their distant mountain hamlets. Squatting in the shade in an abandoned building, young boys in tattered clothes sniffed glue—one way to shut out reality, to silence bad dreams.

Further on, resting on a bed of filthy rags near the gutter, a woman slept with an infant at her breast while an older child, disheveled, wiping an ever-runny nose on her sleeve, begged for alms. And when I chanced upon the *"Basurero,"* the vast, crater-like municipal garbage dump that stretches as far as the eye can see under a blue sky black with vultures, I saw toddlers milling around cardboard abodes that pregnant teens, toothless old women, and cadaverous one-eyed men call home. Dozens sifted through heaps of refuse for a recyclable, salable trinket. Knee-deep in mountains of waste and competing with the odious birds of death, another group of youngsters rummaged for a meal, a slipper, perhaps a discarded toy to brighten an otherwise joyless childhood.

" … Be fruitful, multiply and replenish the Earth."

I asked myself what monstrous sins could these human phantoms have committed to deserve such inexplicable existence. Gliding on the wings of a sudden gust, a crumpled, lipstick-smeared paper napkin landed at my feet. I recognized the gilt monogram of the hotel where the reception had been held the night before. I heard a scream welling in my throat.

Soaring overhead, a squadron of vultures, the ever-present vultures, resumed their abominable vigil, gliding like black-winged demons at a Witches' Sabbath, awaiting death, smelling it, tasting it.

∞

Some 360 kilometers to the east, in Tegucigalpa, I chanced upon a living ghost. Homelessness, a growing scourge on planet Earth, robs people of their identity. Madness, in her case, further sharpens the alienation, the anonymity. She has no name and she will pass in this dimension and from this life unnoticed. Merciful, insanity yanked her from the clutches of her recurring nightmare. But she's real, the symbol and victim of the society that spawned her. Shunned, loathed, she inspires revulsion, not pity, for she is unrepentant, defiant in her grotesque cardboard palace, amid the debris, the scraps of metal, the offal on which she feeds, the useless memories that haunt her still, come rain or come shine, come hell or high water. Ageless, toothless, untamed, and mad, she leans against a wall or steals forty winks on the naked pavement. Wielding a yard of rubber tubing or an old broom, she chases after man and specter, a menacing fist raised against oncoming traffic and snickering children, striking the ground with rage and bewilderment, spitting at passers-by, pelting them with invectives. Sometimes folly crests like an open flame and a torrent of tears drenches her grandmotherly face. Overcome, she quiets down, tunes in briefly on the world around her, a lifeless gaze now focused on an all-consuming void.

One morning, members of the *Fuerza de Seguridad Pública*, Honduras's ham-fisted police, came and destroyed the paper, string, and plastic shelter she'd erected. She put up a fierce battle but the cops prevailed. Trampled by uncaring feet, the decimated remains of her flimsy abode were then carted away.

Up the road, in the narrow, windswept, slop-splattered alley that hugs the flanks of St. Michael's Cathedral, a shadow of a man writhed in drug-induced agony. Foaming at the mouth, his eyes on fire, he crumbled to the ground and let out a blood-curdling shriek. Thrashing about, wallowing in waste, he clawed at the demons that tormented him. Rolling onto the street, he narrowly missed being hit by a passing car. Safe in their pews, their eyes turned heavenward, the faithful basked in the grand spectacle of a mid-day mass. *"Dominus vobiscum,"* chanted the celebrant. *"Et cum spiritu tuo,"* they responded, unmindful of the godlessness that surrounds them.

Around the corner, sprawled on the sidewalk, hoping to squeeze the last traces of pity from a parade of self-absorbed pedestrians, a group of cripples flaunted their grotesque infirmities. Unruffled, the amblers stepped over them like so much rubbish. Across the street, a young woman breast-fed her newborn as three older daughters, sired by three different men, plied the beggar's trade.

Mumbling incoherently, disheveled, froth caking the corners of her mouth, another madwoman exchanged stones and insults with vagrants who taunted her. Sobbing with a studied constancy and resonance, another beggar exposed a newborn at her naked left breast.

Feral dogs, traumatized by hunger, rejection, and loneliness, responded to a friendly whistle or the offer of a caress with sidelong glances filled with sadness, mistrust, fear. Head low, tail tucked between their hind legs, they had surrendered to forces heretofore unimagined, now braved with stoic resignation. They did not have the energy to bark. They waited for the dead of night to unleash their mournful wails.

In the distance, standing legs wide apart in the shade of a big old tree, a policeman gaped catatonically in the void to stay cool, conserve energy, perhaps to guard against the incongruity that surrounded him. On the corner, near the

Excelsior Hotel where I'd spent the night, a man called out: "Anything you want, *hombre*: Dope? Girls? Boys? Name your pleasure."

I point him out to the policeman but he stares at me blankly, his eyes-half shut. He waves me off. It's nearly lunch-time. In the noonday heat even duty takes a siesta.

LIES HIS TEACHER TOLD—Michel Montvert, an art critic I met in Paris on a recent diplomatic mission, doesn't mince words:

"I think, therefore I doubt." He began to doubt, he said, when he "awoke from a blinding sleep and shed the last vestiges of forbearance for senseless beliefs." Nine-tenths of his family had perished in Hitler's gas chambers and the "inscrutability of 'God's' designs," at best an offensive rationale, had since assumed an odious character.[7]

Montvert rejects the notion that Earthlings are born sullied by some "primal offense," that pain ennobles the soul and that, to be saved from sin, sentient beings need to be ruled by an arbitrary system of faith-based doctrines and protocols. In religion's ostensible respectability, Montvert discovered "not a path to enlightenment but an instrument of deceit and emotional bondage."

Montvert's transformation from "fence-straddler to mutineer" had been gradual, filled with misgivings. At first, he found religion's mystique inscrutable.

"I'd meandered through its occluded allegories and bizarre canons like an explorer on a strange, unmapped

---

[7] *His real name is Greenberg.* (Translator)

wasteland. I'd glimpsed the very faint light that religion claims to shed, but found only vast and gloomy shadows.

"It is in the shadows," he said, "that my senses, now accustomed to the darkness, caught sight of a glow, a radiant luminosity that rinsed my pupils free of the gritty debris of credulity. I now understood that blind faith, not truth, prejudice and fear, not common sense, threaten men and enslave them."

Like others before him, Montvert had "absent-mindedly tolerated sundry propositions and viewpoints along the way, some of which I peddled, parrot-like, out of stupidity or intellectual sloth."

Traditional, assembly-line rearing, fashionable in the days of his youth, had instilled a value system that seemed strange if not utterly without merit. Montvert had been coached by otherwise doting parents to defer to authority with robot-like reverence:

"Honor your elders. Venerate your teachers. Obey the boss. Comply with representatives of the public order."

In short, Montvert was to idolize or at least yield to all manner of adults of dubious pedigree who had forgotten what it feels like to look at a very menacing world from three feet off the ground.

In school, Montvert had been programmed by impassive teachers to smile or fight back the tears, to subdue, sometimes smother very raw feelings under the pretext that such comportment is what society expects of a "good little boy" and later, of what Jews admiringly refer to as a *"mensch."*[8] Precocious and sly, Montvert knew that he was not and could never be a good little boy. Nor did he aspire to *menschhood,* a

---

[8] *Decent, honorable man.* (Translator)

reputation not easily conceptualized by a child. But he understood that pretending to be what others anticipate can bring on small rewards or, at the very least, shield one from censure, reprimand or retribution—all of which he eventually incurred when he tired of pretending and transitioned at last from conciliation and neutrality to open defiance.

Later, as his peripheral vision improved and his depth perception deepened, he began to ask questions that would bring scorn and kindle the antipathy of his peers:

• "Why are we susceptible to pain and defenseless against the fury of disasters—natural and manmade—that, religion insists, are wrought against us "for mysterious reasons" by some capricious supernatural force?"

• "Who is this 'maker' who inflicts or tolerates atrocities for 'the good that comes from them'; who orchestrates without apparent aim—or turns a blind eye to—the paroxysms that convulse his realm?"

• "Where is this 'intelligent designer' hiding while the sobs of his creation are never heard?"

• "What 'ineffable' entity is this, whose ear is inattentive and whose arms are so unwelcoming to the throngs who call on him and seek his succor?"

• "What cruel despot decrees that his subjects will speak words not their own, that they will blindly obey the injunctions of self-anointed human go-betweens, that they will tremble at their threats and admonitions, take comfort in their mawkish absolutions, mouth off supplications and requiems, and recite guilt-ridden prayers of indebtedness, veneration, fear, and remorse, all repeated *ad nauseam*, day after day, to a 'God' who never shows his face, never bares his heart, never sheds a tear, never says he's sorry, a 'God' who grants life and, with it, the fear of death?"

The questions, Montvert realized, were in fact declarations conjugated in the interrogative. And crypto-agnosticism turned into atheism.

∞

"This I believe," Montvert offered as we lunched at his favorite *brasserie* on Place de la Nation:

"Religion is divisive, repressive, and irrational. The sectarian hatreds that convulse our planet, the paroxysms of militant religiosity that now grip the world confirm its toxic character."

∞

Karl Marx was right: Religion is the opiate of the people. But unlike opium, which delivers users into a state of blissful, dream-filled lethargy, religion inflames passions and brings out the worst in Earthlings. It is a pathway to discord and, inevitably, to fanaticism, aggression, and war.

∞

A famous French pre-revolutionary political cartoon Montvert displays in his rococo study shows a rakish nobleman and a smiling, overfed clergyman riding on the back of an old, exhausted peasant. The metaphor, pithy and painfully real, may have inspired French philosopher, author, and encyclopedist Denis Diderot (1713-1784) to exclaim:

"Man will never be free until the last king is strangled with the entrails of the last pope."

Flanking the etching, another widely circulated caricature dated 1787 (two years before the storming of the Bastille) shows a monkey *[the king]* asking the fowl in the yard *[the people]* in what sauce they might like to be cooked.

Centuries of oppression by the ruling aristocracy and priestly debauchery would inspire equally pungent anti-religious epigrams by several of Diderot's contemporaries, men celebrated for their intellect, all confirmed agnostics and atheists at a time when agnosticism and atheism were damnable offenses.

Voltaire: *"Every sensible man, every honorable man, must hold religion in horror."*

James Madison: *"Religious bondage shackles and debilitates the mind."*

John Adams: *"This would be the best of all possible worlds, if there were no religion in it."*

Ben Franklin: *"Lighthouses are more helpful than churches."*

Thomas Jefferson: *"Religion is the most perverted system that ever shone on man."*

Thomas Paine: *"Religion is a system of superstition that produces fanatics and serves the purposes of despotism."*

A few years earlier, Jean Meslier, a French Catholic priest who wrote a book denouncing all religions, said *"Newton's infinite space is the only eternal reality. Nothing but matter exists. Religion is a device used by the rich to oppress the poor and render them powerless."*

British lampoonist Jonathan Swift noted, *"We have just enough religion to make us hate but not enough religion to make us love one another."*

Napoleon Bonaparte dismissed religion as *"excellent stuff for keeping common people quiet."*

And writer, philosopher and social commentator, Marquis de Sade, proclaimed: *"Religions are the cradles of despotism."*

∞

It was the despotism and pretense of religion and the vapid snobbery of the nobility that aristocrat Donatien Alphonse-

François, Marquis de Sade, railed against in his seminal oeuvre. And it was the tyranny of historical falsification and the baseness of academic dishonesty that propelled Michel Montvert, an Earthling with a rare and unyielding respect for truth, on a lifelong campaign to exhume it, wherever it might hide. Montvert, whom I first met on a visit to the Louvre Museum (he was admiring "les merveilleuses fesses" *[the marvelous buttocks]* of Boucher's *Odalisque*), also transformed a passion for fine art into a medium through which he would later demonstrate that certain forms of human creativity cry out against lies, injustice and absurd beliefs.

"It began in high school," he reflected. "My history teacher snubbed the French history syllabus and routinely injected his personal prejudices and slanted perceptions."

Armed with "a razor-sharp intellect and a tongue to match," Montvert's teacher was "a fount of erudition, and a skilled pedagogue with a knack for falsification. The broad knowledge he possessed—he was licensed to teach everything from algebra to zoology—was often overshadowed by an appalling lack of objectivity. It was his very scholarship that enabled him, whenever he could, to skew history or to rewrite it by opining about people long dead or by editorializing about events exhaustively chronicled in our otherwise unembellished curriculum."

A royalist at heart *[as are all devout French Catholics]*, Montvert's teacher steadfastly extenuated the arrogance and cruelty of French monarchs by insisting that they were, "good Christians." *[Yes, they retreated to their private gilt chapels and genuflected on ermine stoles and rich brocades while their subjects lived in squalor, tilled their fields, paid exorbitant levies, fought their wars and died of consumption, exhaustion and hunger].*

Distant abstractions, the Crusades and the Inquisition elicited in Monvert's teacher a kind of nostalgic admiration stripped of all misgivings about the horrific crimes committed in their name.

"I remember learning about the events that took place on the night of August 23, 1572, *[the Saint-Bartholomew massacre]* during which 3,000 Huguenots were slaughtered in the streets of Paris on orders of Catherine de Medici. Recapping the incident did not seem to evoke in my teacher any discernible unease."[9]

Injecting personal bias into his instructions, Montvert's teacher presided over his own kangaroo court: "He openly scorned the Huguenot Henri of Navarre, but lavished him with praise when, fearful for his royal neck, the newly-crowned Henri IV converted to Catholicism. *'Paris is well worth a mass,'* the king had sardonically quipped." *[Praise turned to condemnation when the king, now firmly enthroned, issued the Edict of Nantes, a decree restoring religious and political freedom to French Protestants].*

"A few chapters forward, my teacher applauded the edict's revocation, 87 years later, by Henri's grandson, the 'Sun King,' Louis XIV, the archetype warmongering despot whose conceit was eclipsed only by his pomposity."

Unaware of or utterly indifferent to the immense suffering his subjects endured, one of the last of the Bourbon kings, Louis XVI, who spent his reign tinkering with clocks, and his featherbrained wife Marie-Antoinette, who plundered the nation's coffers to keep the court royally entertained, elicited pity and sympathy from Montvert's teacher.

"After all," he never tired of saying, "they were very pious."

As these idiocies were being casually spouted, Montvert would retrieve from the depths of his childhood memories

---

[9] *News of the slaughter would be cheered by King Philip II, who was busy purging Spain of Protestants, Jews, and Moors, and Pope Gregory XIII who, for lack of better things to do, reformed the calendar.* (Translator)

121

Pathé and Fox newsreel footage of priests sprinkling holy water on tanks and cannons and the fuselage of dive bombers so that Christians of one nation could kill other Christians with the full blessings of "Almighty God."

The French Revolution, Monvert's teacher insisted, was "an outrage masterminded by Jewish financiers, Freemasons, degenerate philosophers, and other irreligious libertines." This fictitious depiction was nowhere to be found in the texts Montvert had been issued or in any history book he'd since perused.

∞

The reign of terror that followed the fall of the Bastille on July 14, 1789, was summarily blasted as a "grotesque act of anti-Christian barbarism." Surely, many innocent heads rolled during the two–year frenzy. But Montvert's teacher could not bring himself to admit that the insurrection was the belated [*and cathartic*] aftermath of centuries of misery and oppression or the driving force that would help rid France, for the first time in history, of feudalism, a dissolute clergy, and a mercenary absolute monarchy.

In contrast, the beheading of two royal idlers who bankrupted France while they wined, dined, gambled, "gathered in prayer," made war, and cheered their dogs on helpless foxes, Montvert's teacher insisted, was murder. Nor would he suffer the notion that revolution, as Montvert perilously argued in class, is a process, not an incident. "Many people tend to judge the French Revolution as a single event rather than the culmination of tidal forces whose smallest swells had begun to crest centuries earlier."

In 1789, as the Intergalactic Security Alliance celebrated its tri-millennium, France was a nation of 26 million. French society was made up of three distinct and grossly dissimilar classes: The "nobility of the sword"—some half a million peers of the realm—among them the hereditary "high" aristocracy consisting of 4,000 families, groupies, and bootlickers close to the throne; the petty nobility, composed of provincial gentlemen of lesser means but matching greed; and the *nouveaux-riches*, the coarse *bourgeois* who bought estates and nobility titles but who, despite their wealth, were mocked by the dynastic bluebloods for their miserly origins and vulgar comportment.

The priesthood, 120,000-strong, was also divided between the high clergy (members of the aristocracy) and the common clergy—both degenerate idlers and connivers.

Last was the Third Estate—laborers, farmers, peasants, craftsmen, bankers, lawyers and trades people.

The king's power was absolute, limitless, and issued from "God." The king hired and fired his cabinet at will. All authority was centralized in Paris and in the hands of Louis XVI, a meek and irresolute monarch woefully ill-suited to govern. Injustice, ineptitude, and corruption were rampant.

In 1777, with Lafayette and his volunteers, then in 1779 with Rochambeau and the French Royal Expeditionary Corps, France fought alongside the Americans against the British, culminating in the 1781 victory at Yorktown and the surrender of General Cornwallis. This little adventure, while its poor fed on rats, cost France two billion gold pounds.

This was the twilight of the 18th century, the dawning of "Enlightenment," and France was tired and wary of the ancient and traditional order in which the king is commander in chief, judge, jury, and executioner, a system that called for the aristocracy to defend the nation, the clergy to pray for victory *[while engaging in political intrigue and cavorting with women of ill repute]*, and the rabble to toil and pay crippling taxes until they dropped. Fat and venal, the Church made a mockery of Christian values. The clergy paid no taxes but charged tolls on behalf of the crown and, for a fee, granted indulgences and first-class passage to paradise. Much of the gold they collected and diverted from the royal treasury swelled the personal fortunes of many princes of the Church. Commoners—peasants and bourgeois alike—crushed by unfair and exorbitant tithes, were fuming.

Meanwhile, philosophers, writers, scientists—Voltaire, Diderot, Rousseau, Saint-Simon [*who articulated the principles of socialism*], and Lavoisier [*who established the Law of Conservation of mass, discovered and named oxygen and hydrogen, introduced the Metric system, invented the first periodic table including 33 elements, and helped reform chemical nomenclature*]—saw in revolution a weapon against the despotism of absolute monarchy and the clergy's fanaticism and avarice.

The French Revolution was less an act of insubordination against royal tyranny than a revolt against the social order, inequality, nepotism, and discrimination. It was a populist, not political movement.

The economic crisis sweeping France at the time accentuated the inequality between the classes: As they do now, the rich got richer and the poor sank deeper into poverty. Thousands died of hunger. It was obvious to most that France could not escape mass mutiny. Would it be short or protracted, violent or peaceful? Would essential reforms forestall the inevitable? Only the king, his queen, the blue-bloods, the knights, and the princes of the Church could answer these questions; but they were all opposed to change. People who have enough to eat generally shun the gaze of the poor and the hungry; they do not want to hear the sound of empty bellies.

"I understand the rage Louis and Marie-Antoinette's dehumanizing reign inspired among the people," Montvert sighed. "Everyone is fixated on the royal heads that rolled into the wicker basket but no one gives a damn about the misery of the masses. Royalty is an anachronism, an obscenity."

The French Revolution was an extraordinarily complicated affair. Unlike the American Revolution, which some have likened to an act of defiance by a prodigal son against his overbearing mother, and much like the Russian Revolution, which had already begun to simmer, the French Revolution was a genuine insurrection born of centuries of mismanagement, corruption, oppression, and exploitation of the masses by small, all-powerful, greedy elites. It was a blueprint for liberty and justice that lesser men could not decipher or that they mercilessly corrupted by erecting political monstrosities.

"But my history teacher would have none of that," Montvert grumbled.

THE BONEYARD OF ARROGANCE—The axiom that the world's fate is in the hands of bankers and industrialists is never more fittingly demonstrated than in wartime. The lords of capital and the cannon merchants salivate at the prospect of war. Pillaging the national treasury and fleecing taxpayers, they prosper when the first shots ring out.

And so, military transports will continue to bring home body bags and flag-draped caskets. Posthumous medals will be cast to honor young people who die in unwinnable wars they did not choose to fight. Bugles will play taps and three rifle volleys will ring out in the grief-filled stillness of a hundred village cemeteries. And, until further notice, dubbed the "focal point" of the war on terrorism, Afghanistan, remote, immense, and inhospitable, will continue to thwart efforts to pacify, domesticate, and democratize by military means an enclave throbbing with militant nationalism, deep-seated xenophobia, and religious fervor.

∞

It was in 330 BCE that Alexander the Great, trying to conquer Afghanistan, faced his fiercest battles and greatest losses. He gave up after four years.

Led to believe that they needed to occupy Afghanistan as a buffer against Russia, the British attacked Afghanistan on three separate occasions, and at a devastating cost, between 1838 and 1919.

The Russians invaded Afghanistan in 1979, enduring a nine-year conflict that resulted in catastrophic losses in men and materiel. Five years into the conflict, the Russians were bogged down in a guerrilla war of increasing ferocity. They failed to reduce the insurgency or win acceptance by the Afghan people. Instead, Afghan resistance grew stronger and gained popular support. Fighting spread to all parts of Afghanistan. Soviet airfields, garrisons, and lines of communication, which came increasingly under attack, were ultimately disabled.

A "sanitized" document released by the U.S. Directorate of Intelligence tallies Soviet casualties at about 25,000, including 8,000 dead, and the destruction of more than 600 helicopters, fixed-wing aircraft, and thousands of armored vehicles and trucks.

According to the document, the Afghan army suffered 67,000 casualties; "insurgents" lost some 40,000 men, not including civilian sympathizers. The Soviet program to transform Afghanistan into a reliable client state had no impact. Efforts at media indoctrination of Afghans failed: Most Afghans are illiterate. Fleeting loyalties and sporadic truces were obtained through bribery and deception—a subterfuge the U.S. has admitted to using without success.

"History," Napoleon said, "is the version of past events that people have decided to agree upon." His vast army's debacle on the frozen steppes of Russia in 1812, history agrees, was the result of a fundamental error in judgment: A formidable juggernaut is no match for the courage, selflessness, determination, and patience of stubborn, patriotic people, no matter how militarily outnumbered they might be.

In exile on the island of Elba, reflecting on his losses before escaping, reconstituting an army and taking on the Duke of Wellington at Waterloo, Napoleon quipped, "A leader has the right to be defeated, but never to be surprised."

A century later, Adolf Hitler, a small-time artist and psychopath with a messiah complex who chose surprise over the prophetic nature of past events, emulated Napoleon and invaded Russia. And "General Winter," the redoubtable and invincible strategist that decimated France's Imperial Army *[Napoleon lost more than half a million men]* made short shrift of the Führer's best troops. The mighty Wehrmacht was not equipped for winter warfare, and it underestimated the bravery and fortitude of Soviet troops. Frostbite and disease caused more casualties than actual combat, and the dead and wounded numbered more than 150,000 in the first three weeks of fighting. By the end of the offensive, which was frustrated by tenacious Russian soldiers, more than 1.5 million German soldiers had died.

America's war in Afghanistan, while vastly different from the Napoleonic and German campaigns against Russia, was lost before it ever began owing a dynamic common to both: The U.S. has been fighting against well organized, scrupulously disciplined zealots who know and control the terrain and who, like quicksilver, scatter and disappear into the innumerable chasms, furrows, and crevices that slice through that country's vast mountainous terrain. Add to a lunar topography, deeply rooted religious convictions, a fanatical love of country and an abhorrence of foreign influences which they regard as meddlesome and sacrilegious.

The doubling of U.S. troops in Afghanistan pleased the hawks, the bankers, and the military contractors to no end. It was seen in many quarters as a colossal tactical mistake and another example of economic adventurism that may retard but will not prevent an inevitable and humiliating fiasco.

∞

Dead or alive, Osama bin Laden had been elevated to symbolic eminence. Since his assassination, his message and his mission continue to inspire and galvanize Muslims around the world. It is only when the U.S. awakens from its inflated illusions of military supremacy and moral superiority, and when it sees the world though less myopic and arrogant eyes, that Earthlings can relax long enough to chance what could have been *[but won't be]* the beginning of a meaningful dialogue between a nation long perceived as an imperialist meddler and the rest of the planet.

∞

It is always tempting to attribute the dirty deeds that Earthlings do to "conspiracies." The truth may be more prosaic — a rerun of human nature in the context of unfolding Earth history: Gargantuan egos; unfettered ambition; greed; larceny; a thirst for conquest; a longing for domination, subjugation, supremacy; stealing from the poor to enrich the hyper-rich; ruthless soldiers crowning themselves chief, king, tsar, sultan, president-for-life, caudillo, dictator; clever accountants becoming bankers; wealthy lawyers entering politics to subvert the law, not uphold it; insurance companies practicing medicine; flag-waving cadets aspiring to field command; diminutive corporals dreaming of empire.

What is being replayed is not some dastardly covert scheme by a "chosen few" to rule the world. They rule it already. They always did. They always will. Feudal lords controlled their vassals' lives; slave-owners — their chattels. In theocratic states "spiritual leaders" and the "morality brigades" redefine men's destinies. In some industrialized countries, it's the capitalists at home, the death squads in other people's backyards. In totalitarian states, it's the secret police and the gulags. That's adaptive evolution. Smart, strong-willed, imaginative, ruthless men always claw their way to the top. Others fall by the wayside.

Life itself is a "conspiratorial" biogenic process. Some of it takes place at the atomic level: White cells attack red cells, malignant tumors devour healthy tissue. A permanent change in the DNA sequence causes irreversible mutations. At the macro-political-economic level, elites exploit the masses; the profit-motive eclipses morality. It's in the nature of Earthlings to scheme, conspire, cheat, and, if need be, kill to achieve their aims. Large dinosaurs ate small dinosaurs. Big fish eat little fish. Powerful men make minced meat of lesser men.

Sometimes, as is the case with certain inconvenient truths, imperiled special interests strike back with conspiracy theories of their own. They assert that verifiable, observable scientific phenomena such as global warming are being manipulated to strengthen the argument that human activity affects climate. What they fear in fact is that mounting evidence of man's carbon imprint on nature's delicate balance will weaken states' rights and interfere with "Libertarian" agendas — including the self-granted entitlement to foul the atmosphere with noxious emissions, to dump toxic wastes into rivers and lakes, to genetically modify foodstuffs, and to retard the advent of environment-friendly legislation... because it's good for business.

What Earthlings ought to anticipate is that before a "New World Order" has a chance to dig its fangs deep into their jugulars, a New World *Disorder* will intervene.

Homo hominis lupus. Man is a wolf to man. There will always be lords and there will always be serfs. Some serfs will attempt to usurp their masters' powers. Some will succeed and become lords themselves. Some lords will be deposed and be reduced to servitude. In reasonably free societies, equitable laws protect both the right of lords to hold on to their fiefdoms and that of vassals to be in some way shielded from their lords' excesses. Unfair laws favor one side over the other — generally the lords whose capital, power, and influence *[lobbies and political action committees]* shape those laws. But so long as the peasants have enough to eat and their basic rights to "life, liberty and the pursuit of happiness" are not unduly abridged, the lords will always prevail.

∞

"We're headed for a feudal society consisting of an increasingly smaller group of immensely rich magnates and a gradually larger mass of peons whose primary function is to keep the rich wealthy and to die in their stead on remote battlefields. I saw it coming years ago," Edwyn Wolcott said, shaking a solemn finger. "I also predicted a cataclysmic revolution that would reverse the order of things … but it is not yet in my future or yours. Naturally, after a short period of pointless euphoria, men hungering for power will rise … and the world will be right back where it started. Human history is like a pendulum; it swings back and forth between stifling 'order' and ruinous chaos, between the stagnancy of peace and the intoxicating challenges and rewards of war."

There are no lasting convictions, no immutable doctrines in politics, only temporary accommodations shared by a privileged few who keep manipulating the masses under the pretext that they granted them that right at the ballot box. It was always that way; it always will be so. Earthlings are predatory animals and survival of the fittest is *[still]* the working template.

∞

I was sent to Earth to measure what is left of its fleeting future, not to contradict some of its denizens' gloomy and sadly accurate diagnoses.

IN THE CHILL OF OPEN DISCORD—Meeting this week in Montenegro, the superpowers secretly agreed to wage war for the next 1,000 years or until their empires crumble—whichever comes first. At regular, pre-arranged intervals, heads of state will trade angry words scripted to stimulate the world's adrenal glands. "Police actions," "preemptive strikes," and "limited engagements" will be conducted, as usual, in other peoples' backyards, with or without their consent.

North Atlantic Treaty Organization (NATO) chiefs reiterated that they reserve the right to a first-strike nuclear option to be used anywhere on Earth. Military leaders from the U.S., Britain, Germany, France and the Netherlands released a 150-page blueprint that would draw U.S., NATO and European Union forces together in a "grand strategy" to tackle the challenges of an "increasingly unstable world." Arguing that the West's values and way of life are under threat, the authors of the plan insist that "the first use of nuclear weapons must remain in the quiver of escalation as the ultimate instrument to prevent the *[inevitable]* deployment of weapons of mass destruction." In other words, "we will pulverize you *[and ourselves]* before you have a chance to obliterate us *[and yourselves]* in the process."

An all-out nuclear war, Pentagon strategists reckon, would

destroy urban areas and thereby disable the assets and infrastructures that characterize modern industrial states. This reality, they agree, makes the deliberate launching of such a war the ultimate act of folly. On the other hand, they feel that the U.S., as the self-proclaimed "leader of the free world," should have "credible strategic nuclear options" to offset the no less plausible nuclear options that potential enemies might have devised. This concern has led to debates over the advisability of a "limited" nuclear skirmish that would ostensibly produce significant military results *[and a psychological victory]* but minimal civilian casualties.

At the same time, U.S. policy is being modified to exclude the targeting of "population centers *per se*" — presumably because "collateral" civilian casualties in industrial or military facilities are expected to be much lower than those from direct strikes on population centers. High-mindedness has its devious side.

In the chill of open discord there's always time to prepare for the inevitable. The pact, fiendish in its minimalism, is founded on the premise that war is a morally justifiable deterrent against overpopulation. Thus, creatures that insist on multiplying, in the opinion of generals, economists, bankers, military contractors, and social Darwinists who flocked to the secret Adriatic seaside conclave, threaten the survival of the privileged classes and must periodically be liquidated. Natural disasters, they asserted, are rare, random, and unreliable. What they meant is that "acts of God" lack the cunning and inventiveness of Earthlings' death-dealing capability.

As these palavers took place, representatives of Pacific-rim nations huddled privately in Vanuatu to hammer out the finer points of the Trans-Pacific Partnership (TPP), a pact characterized by one U.S. lawmaker as "a punch in the face of middle class America." Some 600 U.S. corporate lobbyists acting as official advisors are making fateful decisions about jobs and workers' rights, environmental standards, food safety, patents, and intellectual property rights.

The Partnership is much more than a NAFTA-style "free-trade" agreement. It's aimed at making the world safe for corporate investment and insuring extravagant profits by reducing labor costs, undercutting workers' rights, dismantling unions, and emasculating environmental and health regulations that affect revenues. The TPP would govern 40% of U.S. imports and exports. It includes extensive provisions that allow corporations and foreign governments to secretly challenge environmental, labor, financial, consumer protection, and food safety laws. While NAFTA is estimated to have cost the U.S. 700,000 jobs, with another 2.5 million lost due to trade deficits with China, the TPP is projected to cost the U.S. at least one million jobs and further increase the downward pressure on wages.

NAFTA is 20 years old. It's a pact that has had devastating consequences for working families, farmers, indigenous peoples, small business, and the environment. The effects of its extreme investor "rights" clause has been felt far beyond the continent since these "rights," which let corporations sue governments for public policies they don't like, have become a common feature of next-generation trade deals. TPP expands this pro-corporate regime across the hemisphere and the Pacific Ocean. Leaked texts prove the TPP is yet another corporate bill of rights that threatens to destroy livelihoods and accelerate the global race to the bottom in wages and working conditions. TPP provisions enable new corporate attacks on democratically-enacted environmental and consumer-protection legislation. They undermine global economic stability by prohibiting effective regulation of financial markets, reduce access to life-saving generic medications, and increase the cost of prescription drugs.

∞

Whenever people enrich themselves, the gap widens between them and those they leave behind. The story of material progress is one of rising inequality. It is thus hardly surprising that inequality within societies, as well as between them, has become one of Earth's most pressing issues. Many fear that the U.S. is striving to develop social structures resembling those of Latin America where a small, fabulously rich elite faces off against hundreds of millions of people who are denied a ladder into the middle class.

Faced with the inevitable, the well-to-do realize they can never sleep on both ears. The longer they avert their eyes from the suffering of the masses, the greater the loathing they will inspire, the harsher the payback will be. Unmoved by compassion, short on morals, what the elites—in their avaricious pursuit of money—dread is the loss of status and economic security. Those who studied history will dredge up lurid mental images of the raid on the Bastille and the uprisings that dismantled Russia's Tsarist obscenity. They know that, at first, they will be held hostage in their gilded mansions and gated communities. Their estates will then be overtaken by angry mobs of latter-day Jacobins and dirt-poor *muzhiks*, and strung up from the highest trees. Those who mock history or simply regard it as a chronicle of events mummified in the pages of a book will suffer the same fate but without the benefit of hindsight. Thankfully, sometimes justice too is inevitable.

Capitalism, which stratifies humanity according to accident of birth or level of wealth, is not a future-oriented system. It is fuelled by a series of short-term, self-perpetuating schemes designed to wring from the sweat of peons the rewards that privileged classes believe they are entitled to enjoy in the here-and-now. Considering the social and economic ravages capitalism continues to cause around the world, it is an organism, like an imploding star, destined for gravitational collapse. Meanwhile, ignoring the sinister logic of their credo, capitalists and jingoists keep telling each other behind closed doors that only global war can postpone the inevitable.

BATTLEFIELDS & ASSEMBLY LINES—Michel Montvert comes from a culture where the word "God" was never spoken—except as an unprompted exclamation, like *"Merde!"* Nor was death or the hereafter ever discussed, either in a religious or ontological context. He was never given a religious education, nor deprived of such, but the notion of an invisible, omnipotent creator/arbiter/destroyer seemed to him ludicrous even as a child.

By the time he was old enough to understand the magnitude of his parents' suffering, particularly during and right after WWII, their passive belief in deity had turned to agnosticism—his father's early rabbinical studies and his mother's genteel, pseudo-assimilation into a Christian mainstream, notwithstanding. Struck with pancreatic cancer, his mother had endured several months of martyrdom and died, at the age of 59, convinced that religion is a travesty and "God" is a fraud. Heartbroken, his father, a physician, cried out against the fragility of life and the failings of medicine, and spent the rest of his days dissecting and annotating the Bible, not for inspiration but to vilify it, to point to "God's" unfathomable cruelty and draw attention to man's propensity for evil.

"My father and I," Montvert confided, "had long, animated conversations about religion, not in pursuit of an ideological abode but to highlight the contradictions, single out the aberrations. The underpinnings of religion—mysticism, the supernatural, blind faith [*credo ad absurdum, 'I believe because it is absurd,'*] in an unknowable entity, the perfunctory rituals, the taboos and strident proscriptions we agreed—were all contrived to enslave humankind, not liberate it.

"We acknowledged the 'Golden Rule'—the Ethic of Reciprocity—present in Judaism, Christianity, and Islam [*but probably of more ancient Buddhist provenance*] yet we could not ignore man's inclination to disregard it, even violate it, in the name of Yahweh, Theos, and Allah.

"We quoted from Hillel the Elder, the 1st century BCE rabbi who summed up the Torah with the commandment, '*What is hateful to you, do not do to your neighbor.*' We then read Luke (6:31), who teaches, '*Treat others as you want them to treat you.*' Last, we turned to the Koran's lofty counsel, '*No one of you is a believer until he desires for his brother that which he desires for himself*.'"

But "others," "neighbor," and "brother," Montvert and his father understood, have a parochial meaning that, history has shown, refers to "those of our own kind—*us*, not *them*." This would explain the three major religions' susceptibility to intolerance in the service of deity.

Indeed, carried to extremes, religion can render men insane. Only religious fanaticism could inspire a Muslim father to plot the "honor killing" of his own daughter, to bomb a disco filled with Jewish youths [*or slaughter members of a satirical magazine's staff*].[10] Only numinous rapture could lead a self-styled Christian to murder doctors performing legal abortions. Only a Jewish zealot could torch cars on the Sabbath, pounce on members of a peaceful Gay Pride parade

---

[10] *On January 7, 2015, hooded, gunmen killed 12 people, including four cartoonists, at the French satirical magazine Charlie Hebdo in Paris.* (Translator)

and threaten "bloodshed" if the Jerusalem police chief allowed the parade to proceed.

"This is the bare face of religion," Montvert would conclude. "This is how organized religion aims to transform society into a citadel of intolerance and an incubator of fanaticism." The record, father and son concluded, shows that the prime targets of sectarian hatred are "heretics," a one-size-fits-all label that describes those who hold different beliefs than one's own, or who grant themselves the inalienable right to hold none. Within that conflict rests the unresolved tension between the command to love one's enemies and the equally strong injunction to reject any alien or divergent dogma.

In the final analysis, neither Jew, nor Christian, or Muslim knows which of the two commands to follow at any given time. By attacking "heretics" as tools of Satan, religious extremists seize the rhetorical high ground and shift the focus from loving one's enemies to the escapist option of waging war against an imaginary source of iniquity. This was the preeminent rationale for millennia of senseless bloodshed.

"There are no lasting convictions in politics, only temporary accommodations shared by a privileged few who manipulate their subjects' destinies under the pretext that they granted them that right at the polls," Montvert exclaims. "Democracy is not a defensible system. Not in the long run. Athens crumbled, victim of domestic wars and patrician greed. Corruption and irreparable political divisions extinguished the Roman republic. Democracy's noblest attributes, the ideals it purports to champion, the very freedoms it promotes — all enfeeble it because it tolerates in its bosom the existence of undemocratic ideas and the proliferation of repressive institutions. In so doing, democracy sows the seeds of its own demise. The more capricious the freedoms we wrest, the more we abuse them. Think of an organism whose parts, in order to survive, conspire against the whole; picture Medusa devouring itself. It's a mesmerizing spectacle. The symbiosis is fatal in the end."

"So what's left," I ask.

"Uncertainty. The thrill of impermanence. Randomness. Bedlam. Choose your poison. Rebels and despots trade places until it's impossible to tell them apart. Earth will continue to produce would-be redeemers bent on saving humanity — or else. The spider will spin her web, the sun will rise, the cockerel will proclaim the birth of a new day, and we will spurt out of our mothers' bellies, wet and cold, destined to thrash about for a time on battlefields and assembly lines, while the tax collector.... One thing is clear. We are selfish. We suffer from selective amnesia and rarely learn from our mistakes. Life is absurd. Death comes all too soon."

∞

Earth's history is written and redacted by Earthlings. Stripped of their biases, inferences and omissions, history is little more than a mind-numbing compendium of names, events and dates. But things have changed since the advent of live news coverage. History now unfolds in real time and Earth's social scientists view it as an evolution from savagery to sophistication. But members of the Intergalactic Security Alliance are far less upbeat. Earthlings struggle; they live in fear, turmoil, and madness. They want to impeach the cretins, the killers and the kleptocrats they elect, but they neglect to denounce their own stupidity.

Yes, victors blue-pencil history to justify and exalt conquest, losers to blunt defeat. The hostility such disagreement invites often leads to other assaults, other defeats.

Life drives Earthlings mad. But they keep on feigning sanity. It helps dress up their lives. If acting is the art of pretense, living is the science of deceit. They do a bit of both now and then, and sometimes it's hard to tell which is which. Humankind can't tolerate itself so it keeps on procreating. It's a form of mutual chastisement. Life feeds upon the innocent. The supply is inexhaustible.

Montvert accepts with equal dispassion both the wretchedness and the sublime transcendence of the human spirit. Leaning against the forged iron railing of his balcony, surrounded by window-boxes brimming with zinnia, geranium, and petunia, he gazes at his beloved Paris. Then scenes from his childhood blur the exquisite scenery.

June 14, 1940. The Germans had crossed the ancient city gates. Huge flags — a black swastika on a field of crimson and white — towered over palaces and public buildings. Paris had been overpowered. A ghastly silence hovered over the once bustling narrow cobbled streets of the old part of town. It was as if the city had lost its soul. Elsewhere, on Place Pigalle, on the Champs Elysées, in the open vastness of the Place de la Concorde, small groups of Parisians, including priests, greeted and feted the invaders. Many volunteered their services. Others offered their bodies for bread or wine or money to expiate France's fervid capitulation in a symbolic act of self-immolation.

Montvert also remembers seeing vast numbers of Parisians standing motionless, weeping openly, a quiet rage burning in their eyes as German soldiers — the reincarnated Sons of Darkness — strutted freely in the sublime but now dimmed City of Light. He would never forget their tears. Nor could he ever forget taking his father's hand and huddling next to him for warmth and reassurance. Sensing disquiet, his father had picked him up and held him in his arms. He had smiled and pressed him closer to his heart, and Montvert had seen sadness in his father's face; sadness and fear.

Montvert was three.

Michel Montvert is now an old man. Time has done little to quiet the inner echoes of primal cynicism that had escorted him since childhood. He has sailed the seven seas, flown on the Concorde, scaled Mayan tabernacles, probed the Kabbalah's dizzying and mazelike realm, marveled at the erotic carvings of the Khajuraho temples in India, dived in the amethyst waters of the Gulf of Aqaba, combed the ruins of the ancient Essene community in Qumran, pored over the ancient scrolls.

There are fundamental questions that Earthlings must come to terms with if they are to take their subjective existence seriously, among them death, the meaning of life and the place or absence of "God" in that equation. Conscious reality is very complex. Because their lives seem to lack an "objective" or universally quantifiable value, Earthlings create value by talking about it, by philosophizing. Intrinsic meaning exists in the universe, but Earthlings are incapable of finding it because the human brain is still evolving, because it is as yet unable to fathom itself. Thus, for the time being, Earthlings will have to cope with the absurdity of their existence and accept its utter incomprehensibility. They do that best by trivializing it.

AN AMUSING LITTLE ACRONYM—Few things are as predictable as the fickleness of Earthlings. And so another war has erupted, this time too close for comfort. The prognosis is poor.

It all began with a salvo of veiled threats and backhanded rejoinders tailored to help adversaries save face at home while giving the rest of the world the impression that a global conflagration was inevitable unless one side or the other relented. Growing levels of conflict, terrorism, and the toppling of regimes in the Middle East and Africa, as well as political violence in East Asia, had been fueling political instability worldwide. Since 2010, one in ten countries has experienced a significant increase in political volatility. Governments have asserted control over natural resources; regimes are being ousted by popular uprisings; investors face expropriation. Unrest is being blamed on the erosion of freedom, increasing crackdowns on dissent, the brutality of security forces against demonstrators and soaring food prices. In the West, the impact of the global financial crisis has resulted in high unemployment. This, combined with austerity measures, has contributed to growing inequality and stalling or declining living standards. Political landscapes in Europe and the U.S. are becoming fragmented and polarized as populist parties flourish in response to growing voter frustration.

While Earthlings aimed to forge durable agreements to prevent certain countries from developing a single nuclear weapon, they ignored a far greater danger—the myriad weapons already poised against potential threats. Nearly 20,000 nuclear warheads are now geared up to strike. They pose an ongoing existential threat to human survival that has largely been ignored since the Cold War ended nearly three decades ago. The humanitarian consequences of even a limited nuclear war, such as a conflict in South Asia between India and Pakistan involving just 100 Hiroshima-size bombs, would put two billion people's lives at risk. The local effects would be devastating: Explosions, firestorms, and radiation would kill more than 20 million people. But the global repercussions would be far worse. The firestorms would loft five million tons of toxic particulate matter high into the atmosphere, blocking out sunlight and causing temperatures to plummet across the planet. Climatic disruptions would also cause a sharp worldwide drop in food production. There would be a 15% decline in U.S. corn production and a 17% decrease in Chinese rice harvests, both lasting a decade or more. A staggering 33% falloff in Chinese winter wheat production could last for more than 15 years. The resulting global famine would imperil some 900 million Earthlings in the developing world who already suffer from malnutrition, and 400 million people living in countries dependent on food imports. In addition, the huge shortfalls in Chinese food production would threaten another 1.5 billion Earthlings within China. At the very least, there would be a decade of social and economic chaos in the world's largest country, home to the planet's most dynamic economy and bristling with a huge nuclear arsenal of its own.

A nuclear war of comparable magnitude anywhere on Earth would produce the same global impact. By way of comparison, each U.S. Trident submarine carries 96 warheads, each ten to 30 times deadlier than the weapons used in the South Asia scenario. The U.S. has 14 of these stealthy juggernauts, plus land-based missiles and a fleet of strategic bombers. The Russian arsenal has the same incredible overkill capacity.

Taken as a whole, and unless the world economy ushers in a sustained recovery and nuclear weapons are eradicated, it is not premature to assert that Earth has entered an era of irreversible upheaval.

∞

War is a lucrative pursuit, especially for the warmongers, but it is often the result of miscalculation, not design. No sane being really wants war, and none is quite prepared to wage it, let alone win it. In time, the words got sharper, less oblique, and weapons, the antithesis of reason, grew deadlier with each official sound bite. A number of wise men whose opinion no one sought suggested that the capacity to annihilate one another dissuades rivals from slugging it out, thus justifying the escalation of that capacity to its *nth* degree. They revived an old moniker: *Mutually Assured Destruction*. MAD for short. Everyone found it an amusing little acronym. Few get the message.

Other wise men likened hatred to an energy that cannot be compressed indefinitely and which must be vented from time to time, thus making war a routine if somewhat inelegant necessity, like farting. Subconsciously, humans crave war, they argued. The only way to create peaceful societies, they reckoned, is to wipe out a large number of people. Catharsis or reflex, war helps relieve the unbearable burden of having to fake civility in a world cyclically humbled by ignorance, vulgarity, and sadism. Wired as he is, they said, the "naked

146

ape" cannot forever repress his homicidal instincts. He needs a user-friendly outlet for his wickedness. Fantasizing is not enough.

And so the rhetoric of war spiraled in tone and intensity. No one protested very loudly. Not a single voice rose against the demagogues who beat the drums of war. No one dared send to hell the politicians who cheer it on, the economists who rationalize it, the bankers who finance it, the industries that thrive on it and the generals who prosecute it — while young imbeciles are forced-marched to the front to die, be maimed or rendered insane in the name of "national security." Even the dissenters kept quiet, their gray matter anesthetized, their vocal cords deadened by fear or waning conviction. It felt as if a malignant tedium, a pervasive apathy had overtaken them.

Much maligned, Samuel Huntington is at long last being vindicated: When dissimilar ideologies collide or hegemonic interests diverge, pitting cultures against one another, conflicts erupt. The wars that now thunder across the globe confirm the Harvard scholar's thesis. On one hand, Western *[chiefly American]* political arrogance, and the interplay between Russia's hegemonic designs and China's manifest objective to introduce a form of controlled capitalism within its bulging borders on the other are carving a widening rift between ideological opposites. Earth is now being singed by the glowing embers of rising Islamic self-identity and the explosion of religious fanaticism. Earthlings are on the eve of a great religious war and dawn is nowhere in sight.

Torn by decades of civil strife, corruption, widespread

poverty, and vanishing civil liberties, Central and South America fell first, like gangrenous limbs, in an orgy of blood-letting that turned the rivers red and the fields into open graves. Power-starved Latin American colonels and corrupt puppet civilian regimes installed by the Central Intelligence Agency are feeding popular discontent and fomenting disturbances that they are then ordered to crush.

In the Balkan's tender underbelly, self-absorbed, caught up in ethnic violence, Serbs, Croats and Bosnians have restarted a war they no longer recognize and do not have the courage to end. A neologism, "ethnic cleansing," deceptively sterilized, horribly banal, fails to attenuate the barbarism it evokes.

Southeast Asia is crumbling under the weight of its own spectacular, if short-lived, economic gigantism. Unable to trade with impoverished client states and spurned by former political partners, a hastily formed triumvirate between South Korea, Singapore, and Taiwan has collapsed.

Tribal war and AIDS in Africa's heartland add new resonance to the word *holocaust*. Sikhs, Hindus, and Muslims — all convinced of the purity of their creed — are setting fire to a subcontinent devoured by illiteracy, poverty, class divisions, malnutrition, and disease. And in the "Holy Land," against all holiness and wisdom and compassion, fear, distrust, and hatred make a mockery of the "God" the Jews invented, the Christians paganized, and the Muslims, who haphazardly contrived an Arab version of Judaism, conscripted and armed to the teeth.

Bloated and bursting at the seams, China has overrun eastern Siberia, Japan, the Indochina peninsula, and Afghanistan. Planning for the inevitable, it is rounding up and torturing dissidents while the swastika is being resurrected and hailed in a "new" Germany disfigured first by partition then forced reunification.

Isolated and moribund, five former Soviet Republics have collapsed in a final spasm of paranoia.

Nonaligned to the bitter end, Canada, the last vestige of Britain's long dissolved commonwealth, joined Iceland, Sweden, Norway, and Finland in a sub-Arctic neutrality pact that excluded the U.K. and tied up vital sea lanes through the North Sea.

In the Middle East, the predictable collapse of a shaky 40-year alliance between two Arab States, a territorially partitioned semi-autonomous Palestine and their perennial enemy, Israel, opened a third front. Militarily worn out and economically drained after decades-long attempts to impose its will on other countries, its disregard of international law and unilateral use of force, the U.S. has abandoned Israel to its fate. Willful and incorrigible, now armed with nuclear, biological, and chemical weapons, Iran, Syria, and Libya stand poised to launch their long-range surface-to-surface missiles.

Out of spite, not strategy, Greece reclaimed Cyprus. It then pounced on Turkey. Turkey retaliated, pulverizing Athens and the port of Piraeus.

Dismembered, reduced to rubble by tribal and religious strife, Iraq, America's second Vietnam, is smoldering. Thirteen Earth years ago, a fraudulently re-elected president had bulldogged America into an undeclared, costly, unpopular, bloody, and unwinnable war premised on erroneous [and counterfeit] assumptions against an enemy fathered and long coddled by the U.S. Saddam Hussein, it will be remembered, was Uncle Sam's "Man in Baghdad" until he defied his puppet master. No one flinched in America when "the Beast of Tikrit" massacred thousands of his own people. A dozen warlords, each with an ax to grind, now control small enclaves of half-starving "supporters" and the debacle lingered on as the U.S. allowed itself to be dragged into another Middle Eastern skirmish that dangerously compromised its military capital and lay waste to America's economy.

As the U.S. spread thin in a number of military operations, Russia, which had itched to humble the U.S. in the early stages of the Cold War and never gave up its desire to chasten the "paper tiger," seized the moment and reasserted itself by forging a Stalin-Ribbentrop-style non-aggression alliance with China and North Korea. Russia has nothing to lose should the U.S. eventually "decline and fall" — on the contrary. Stirred by an ancient longing and mortified that it never recovered from the breakup of its vast empire, which it considers "the greatest geopolitical catastrophe of the 20th century," Russia is now weighing its options and smugly eyeing a disintegrating world. Kremlin strategists are convinced that Western Europe will blink and do nothing to intervene.

Russia also knows that the U.S. has lost much of its prestige, preeminence, and economic clout; that its infrastructures are crumbling, that it is being increasingly isolated and that the number and fanaticism of her foes is swelling with every acidulous pronouncement by certain members of Congress. In response to America's anti-ballistic program, Russia had been rebuilding the most formidable arsenal of nuclear warheads in the world. North Korea, a sworn enemy of the U.S., possesses a number of nuclear weapons and state-of-the-art delivery systems. Much of Western Europe, now weaned from NATO and pursuing its own aims through the European Union, continues to show alarm at and displeasure with the turn of events in Iraq and Afghanistan. Islamic nations, fundamentalist and secular — such as Turkey — have been more vocal than ever in their hatred of the U.S. New terrorist cells are springing up around the world as antipathy mounts against globalization and in response to the not-too-farfetched perception by Muslims that the U.S. has an anti-Islamic imperialistic agenda.

Africa, still smarting from 500 years of colonialism and resentful of America's historic indifference toward it, has turned bitterly anti-western, anti-white. The South African blood bath, long prophesied but never forestalled, even after the abolition of apartheid, erupted like a pustule, inflaming contiguous states and storming through the continent from the Cape of Good Hope to the Mediterranean, from the Indian Ocean to the Atlantic.

Halfway around the world, Australia is on full alert, if as yet uncommitted, awaiting the results of an emergency plebiscite in New Zealand calling for the dissolution of a non-aggression pact between the two nations.

South of Vera Cruz, from the Pacific to the Yucatan, Mexico's truncated Tehuantepec Isthmus is now in the hands of drug cartels. Northern states, their economy in shambles, have been hastily granted U.S.-protectorate status. Overwhelmed by a tidal wave of undocumented migrants, the U.S. has long since become Mexico's de facto economic custodian. While draining its meager and dwindling resources, this concession helped the U.S. line its southern flank with an extra layer of protection *[provided by forcibly conscripted Mexicans]* against the rebel onslaught. It is just a matter of time.

Sunnis and Shi'a are killing each other. Palestinians threaten yet another intifada over public works projects at sites "holy" to Jews, Christians, and Muslims along the Jordan River and in Jerusalem *[where ultra-Orthodox Judaism has been Talibanized]*.

∞

Episodic at first, famine is now spreading like wildfire. Infant mortality has reached pandemic levels. There are other casualties. What little food can be scraped to keep the heart pumping is proving less than adequate to nourish the brain. Over three billion people suffer irreversible brain damage. Asylums are full. More are desperately needed to contain a swelling tide of insanity but none is being built and the overflow has spilled into streets, along with the homeless, the sick, the dead, and the dying.

After 60 years of regional skirmishes, no one knows for sure why this war is being waged. Nor can anyone remember why these all-consuming conflicts had erupted in the first place. The belligerence of the warring factions has not abated but the cost of maintaining troops and materiel has skyrocketed, prompting each side to further slash domestic programs while raising taxes and artificially deepening inflation,

Things aren't much better in the U.S. where I may have overstayed my welcome and severely strained my patience. Once called the beacon of freedom, the cradle of justice, more pompously hailed as the Land of Opportunity and the Garden of Earthly Delights, the U.S. is being sucked into a black hole of decadence that exposes the depraved priorities of a country that sold its soul to a handful of billionaires. Some 15% of Americans, or about 50 million people, live at or below the official "poverty level." More than 11 million people are without work and millions more have exhausted their unemployment benefits. Some 20 million Americans are classified as illiterate.

The U.S. has the world's largest prison population. Incarcerated in private penal complexes whose custodial responsibilities do not include rehabilitation, re-humanization, and reintegration into society, most inmates are black and Hispanic. Minorities are more likely to be profiled, stopped, frisked, arrested — often with excessive force — summarily tried, convicted, and executed. Nearly one in ten is behind bars. Lax gun laws, vigilantism, rising racial disparities in wealth and income, the militarization of police, and racism continue to disfigure an America whose thick theatrical maquillage is rapidly peeling off.

TO PROTECT & SERVE—A rank, sulfurous halo hangs low over Manhattan. Driven by icy gusts, tentacle-like fingers of swirling amber gases swoop toward the slime-slick pavement, probing deep into yawning doorways, arcades and atria, seeking out the specters that lurk within their drafty expanse.

It's Christmas Eve in the "Big Apple." Chiming in the distance in pious unison, ethereal and uninvolved, church bells summon the faithful. Chiming? No, *tolling*—a lugubrious knell for the erstwhile greatest city on Earth, now a swarming, moribund metropolis, for the faceless night creatures that haunt its streets, for the living dead that NYPD Sgt.-Detective Joe Krolick gets paid to hunt down and kill.

It all came together when politicians, anxious to save face and give voters the impression that justice was being served, let the long simmering rancor, the restive hatred burst like an ugly abscess. Violence, sporadic and extemporaneous at first, grew bolder and deadlier with each secret municipal emergency meeting.

No one complained. Not a single cry of horror was ever heard. It was too late. Justice, *[like truth]*, the stronger of two conflicting arguments; justice, the paradox teetering on the tip of a sword, put on its most fearsome face. The Lady took off the blindfold and winked lasciviously at the oligarchs. And the carnage began.

'Tis the season of all folly, *falalalala* ... and the blood of the expendable, young and old, thinner than water, coalesces with the putrid rivulets of swill and excrement that hug the curb and cascade into the storm drains.

Torn by crime, soaring unemployment, triple-digit inflation, and homelessness, suffocated by Orwellian federal statutes, New York is putrefying and crumbling like the toes of a leper.

As the chasm between rich and poor widens, ever-growing numbers of affluent urban dwellers are moving out to escape the squalor, the soaring taxes, the violence, and the decaying infrastructures. The exodus is turning cities and towns into tracts of depravity, disease, and social unrest.

For every child who wakes up poor and hungry, another dies of neglect or abuse. One-parent families are now the norm, each producing its quota of juvenile offenders. More than four million minors are in custody on charges ranging from truancy and drug possession to petty theft and prostitution. Two million more are serving hard time for capital crimes, including murder, rape, aggravated assault, armed robbery, and home invasion. Most are caged with hardened adult felons — ten to a cell. There is no more room.

Sparked by a rising demand for slave labor and conscripts, immigration from the Third World keeps adding to the ranks of the poor, the marginally educated, and the culturally estranged segments of society. Many future felons start out as street children. Most of the minors who live on the streets and in the catacombs and sewers beneath subway and railroad tunnels suffer from mental disorders. Drug-induced dementia and a form of early Parkinsonism, blamed on raging air and water pollution, afflict thousands of others. Thousands more have perished at the hands of self-styled avengers, sexual psychopaths, and state-sponsored death squads, all dispensing their brand of justice. There are just too many kids out there.

Inexplicably, in one last spasm of puritanical fervor, bolstered by an apostate Supreme Court and a Church obsessed with the unborn but indifferent to the living, "pro-lifers" have at last succeeded in reversing *Roe vs. Wade* and in making abortion a federal crime punishable by death. The oligarchs must be assured a steady supply of cheap labor; the Church a steady supply of dues-paying penitents.

Sgt.-Detective Krolick gets paid to pluck the decaying fruits of this incestuous union.

Byron is 13, clever, resourceful. Krolick's been shadowing him for nearly a week, clambering up and down the side streets and alleyways the boy and his cronies scour in search of shelter or easy prey — old folks stranded in the night.

Midnight. Christmas is hailed with spontaneous acts of vandalism and drunken displays of nudity. There is little cheer. Off of Eighth Avenue, behind the Port Authority Bus Terminal's mazelike network of ramps and underpasses, a band of nine- and ten-year-olds take turns scrounging through trash bins and peeking through the windows of a dingy motel where couples come to risk procreation in exchange for the shallow reward of a brief grunt of pleasure. A block away, a pedophile barters with a twelve-year-old. Envious and resentful, four urchins encircle and pounce on their competitor.

It's now 2:50 a.m. Leaning against a pile of cardboard boxes by the wharf, near the old Fulton Fish Market, Byron is hallucinating. It could be glue or crack or the new rage in town — stalactites — a deadly blend of acetone-imbibed cannabis and over-the-counter decongestants. Byron is said to be armed and dangerous.

Byron spots Krolick. He freezes. Krolick unsheathes his revolver and aims it at Byron, slowly, assertively, with the poise granted Earthlings whose conscience is stilled by the exigencies of job and duty. Mockingly, Byron spreads his arms in Christ-like fashion, resting his head against his shoulder. He smiles. Defiance, stoicism, relief are all etched in his life-hardened baby face, in those glassy eyes where night's eerie scintillations shimmer. He looks at Krolick without rancor, a martyr without a cause, a sacrificial lamb whose sacrifice brings about no redemption. Krolick squeezes the trigger, repeatedly, remorselessly, grateful that another street child, alone and hungry since birth, abused and abandoned by his family, mistreated by his peers, another boy nobody smiles at, nobody cuddles, nobody protects, nobody comforts, nobody loves, will never again sully the society that begat him.

Childhood is when the future begins. Death is when memories expire. Byron never had a future. Krolick revoked his past. "It's a living." Krolick shrugs his shoulders. He must not philosophize. He's just obeying orders. *To protect and serve.* The price of a family Christmas dinner keeps going up. "Thank God for overtime," he muses as he slides his gun back in its holster.

A MIRE OF FOUL MATTER & BLOOD—Men 17 to 69 are in uniform, training for the front or patrolling the streets. Everyone is armed. The haves wrangle with the have-nots. Looting, assaults, and other spasms of violence soared during the long hot summer and thousands died at the hands of paramilitary squads, mercenaries, and gangs, all eager to settle scores. Justice is blind to injustice. Anti-war activists have been on the attack. All they achieved was to foment greater resentment against their cause by flag-waving diehards too old to be conscripted but misguided enough to raise the decibels of jingoism and sanctimony to ear-blasting heights.

Basic staples—bread, milk, eggs—are in short supply. Meat, oh what a horror, when available at black market prices, is rarely fresh. But hunger subverts reason and everyone takes chances. And while hunger and exposure kill the poor, it is often food poisoning that claims those who can still afford to eat.

Not unlike ants, people spent the fall hoarding and digging in deeper. A calamitous winter, at best, lies ahead.

∞

At Universal Press International, where Edwyn Wolcott

works, dispatches and wire service reports keep a skeleton crew on its collective toes. Wolcott had double-shifted for over four months, shuttling back and forth between decoding room and rewrite desk. If the newsgathering team can no longer manipulate events, the editor had decreed, they will milk them down to the last drop. In times of great upheaval, the press will often sacrifice the sacred duty to enlighten for the intimate joy of giving the public palpitations. Anything to sell news. Anything.

Wolcott had spent nearly a lifetime publishing articles in which he had steadfastly kept the emperor naked for all to see in his shameless nudity. His exertions had produced short-lived, insignificant ripples, not the tsunami of revulsion his polemics were intended to unleash. For humanity to survive and thrive, he had insisted, the radical ideas of one generation must eventually become the common sense ideas of the next. At 70, Wolcott had come to the conclusion that "the more we probe within ourselves, the more certain we become of the unreality of temporal free will. The only freedom we really possess is the contemplation of untested ideas and the consequences they trigger."

Telling inconvenient truths is risky business. Wolcott knew. He'd been in the trenches as tracer bullets whizzed over his head. He'd been grazed once or twice. Had his reflexes failed him when he exposed political corruption, police brutality, and military crimes, he might not be whining today.

Much still begged to be said, revealed, dissected. Wolcott had been tempted to veer away from truths that infuriate readers and treat them instead to the kind of bland fiction that spares them the hazards of hypertension. "Tempted but never overcome," he'd sworn.

Words survive briefly in the two-dimensional realm of an investigative report or opinion piece, but they fail to generate change. Instead, they leave a wasteland of rhetoric that does nothing to alter human nature, chill passions, and curb hatred. Some horrors are simply too shocking or too banal for words.

The truth is not a marketable commodity. Wolcott had abandoned all pretenses that his columns would ever stimulate a rational dialogue, let alone trigger change. Resorting to disinformation, a phalanx of right-wing moralizers who hide behind the anonymity of their blogs always struck back, rejecting facts or trivializing them with puerile, spiteful ad-hominem assaults.

Is truth-telling worth the wall of odium and discord it raises? Wolcott struggled with this question with every commentary he penned. "If it takes whining to ventilate inconvenient truths, so be it. I will whine. It helps clear my throat."

∞

George Edwyn Wolcott lost more hair today. More teeth fell out. His gums are dissolving. Droplets of blood ooze from the corners of his eyes. He feels no pain, only overpowering, unrelenting fatigue. These are "premonitory symptoms," says the Federal Emergency Management Agency. The language of disaster is so antiseptically vague. Neutron and gamma rays work slowly. But they kill in the end.

It had all started with an argument over whose god was more amiable, compassionate and merciful. The end came a little after eight, on a dusky, moonless night when a second laser-triggered blast ignited the sky 10,000 meters above Earth. Electromagnetic pulses set off a massive chain reaction that silenced all communication satellites and knocked out power from pole to pole, from zenith to nadir, from first meridian east to first meridian west. The conflagration released direct ionizing and thermal radiation in the infrared and ultraviolet spectra and unleashed hurricane-force winds. The thermal pulse kindled firestorms that coalesced into a mass inferno. The high overpressure and cyclonic airstreams that accompanied the blast upsurge collapsed buildings, crushing and trapping people and exposing them to flying debris in a radius of 300 miles. Ruptured gas lines, spilt fuels, and electrical short circuits widened the fires kindled by thermal radiation. The initial fireball lofted radioactive dust and ash into the thermosphere, causing deadly lightning-induced electron precipitation. The residue floated back to earth in a matter of days. An estimated 42 million Earthlings died in the aftermath.

As I survey the devastation, I am reminded that planet Earth was always a place where some have more than anyone could ever need to live with dignity, while others have nothing. It's a realm in which good and evil are so hotly contested and so narrowly intertwined, where right and wrong feed upon each other with such voracity that neither wins nor loses so that both may emerge unscathed from their unholy symbiosis. It's a setting where the old call upon the young to risk mutilation and insanity or to die in their stead in the name of murky ideals. It's a spot where wars are waged to break the monotony of peace, where combatants are feted for their homicidal deeds with medals and ribbons and boisterous parades, whereas common killers rot in stinking jails or swing from the gallows. It's the halfway house where, left to their own devices, flawed but redeemable beings mutated into a race of cutthroats. It's the purgatory where a race of erect bipedal primates was exiled a quarter of a million years ago so that they might expiate their brutish ways. For you see,

Earthlings are not of "Earth." You hail from a faraway planet known as Khokhma[11], an enchanted sphere that is equal parts matter and essence, intellect and emotion, form, measure, infinity and perpetuity; an abode where inexplicable cosmic forces are revealed; where ideas that come from nowhere are given substance; where the intellectual power of the soul turns potential into actuality, imaginable life force into the Infinite Light.

∞

Then, from the wings, I saw the heavens part. And the glow lingered for days. A great stillness visited upon the realm. Survivors embraced and shed tears of shame and atonement, and they spoke of turning swords into plowshares. And a thousand score and ten passed. But lo and behold, the women ceased to bear fruit and the men became ill with madness and took daggers to their own hearts to smite the evil that festered within. And from the fertile Plains of Lomakhom to the icy peaks of Ephess, from the distant shores of Khlum to Ein's ethereal summits, there was not a voice, not a murmur, not a thistle, not a single blade of grass. Instead, emptiness reigned, vast, final. Time has stood still.

∞

Those who claimed that "the end of the world isn't what it used to be," that a "nuclear winter which would usher a life-extinguishing arctic night" is a myth that was laid to rest *[like global warming]* in the potter's field of liberal doomsday

---

[11] *Named after the driving force in the creative process; the ability to look deeply at some aspect of reality till one succeeds in uncovering its underlying axiomatic truth.* (Translator)

predictions, are regurgitating their words, along with their rotting viscera.

Somewhat less immersed in his patrician past, eager against all hope for comforting news, Wolcott, who'd been listening to The Beatles' *All You Need is Love* when the world collapsed around him, spends his waking hours huddled by the radio. Short-wave transmissions are ebbing, except for hysterical recitations by half-crazed preachers who seem to be gloating at the calamities they'd been longing for:

> *"All ye blasphemers shall be hanged by the tongue until it cleaves and forks like that of a snake. Women who adorn themselves for the purpose of adultery shall be suspended by the hair over a pool of broiling magma. The men who knew them shall be hung by their testicles and their heads lowered slowly into the pool of lava. Doubters and nonbelievers shall be cast in a pit of creeping things that will torment them. Men who take on the role of women in a sexual way and women who take on the role of men shall be dragged up a great cliff by angry angels, and hurled to the bottom. They will then be forced up it, over and over again, ceaselessly, to their doom. Women who had life ripped out of their bellies shall be thrust up to their necks in a lake formed from the blood and gore that issued from their loins. They shall forever be tormented by the spirits of their unborn children. And those who performed the abortions shall spend eternity wading in a mire of foul matter and blood...."*

Wolcott will be spared the demented chatter when his batteries run out.

Last I heard the snows of the Himalayas had vaporized. The mighty Amazon has run dry. Plutonium showers are expected to drench the Sahara tomorrow. Nature repays Earthlings' disregard for it with justifiable contempt. Perhaps George Edwyn Wolcott and Michel Montvert and NYPD Sgt.-Detective Joe Krolick know that by now. Perhaps they'd watched the spasms that convulse their world and perhaps they'd distractedly shaken their heads, aware that all the tumult and misery and violence could have been avoided if only their fellow humans had not been so prone to stupidity, egotism, greed, and irrationality, if their lust for life had not somehow been genetically sabotaged by some brutish collective death wish.

Perhaps is such an empty word.

AFTERWORD

Isaiah commands: *"Learn to do right; seek justice. Defend the oppressed. Take up the cause of the fatherless; plead the case of the widow."* Luke affirms that *"Whoever yearns for freedom, justice, and peace may rise again and raise his head, for in Christ liberation is drawing near."* The Quran teaches: *"Allah forgives all sins. Truly, He is Most Forgiving, Most Merciful."* And the Code of Hammurabi, which precedes them all, vows to *"bring about the rule of righteousness in the land, so that the strong should not harm the weak."*

Somehow, these ancient pleas and reassurances turned out to be hollow, cruel hoaxes. Moses' ten simple directives are habitually, maliciously violated. The "Savior" saved nothing. Allah forgives only those who believe in him. Convulsing under rising waves of ignorance, hatred, and stupidity, racked by mounting violence, planet Earth still awaits salvation— from itself. In defiance of half-hearted warnings by the "First World," crippled by poverty, gloom, and ethnic strife, and sundered by shifting loyalties, "developing nations" indulge in genocide. Generation after generation, yearning for social justice, economic equilibrium, and independence from their puppet masters, lurching from restlessness to inertia, they teeter on the brink of civil war, or have succumbed to it. In other parts of the world, Earthlings struggle to preserve increasingly shrinking fragments of their ancestral homelands. Global warming is putting polar regions on thin ice and threatens to inundate coastal areas and engulf dozens of islands around the globe. Warning that artificial intelligence could one day wipe out the human race, physicist Stephen Hawking writes,

> *"One can imagine AI outsmarting financial markets, out-inventing human researchers, out-manipulating human leaders, and developing weapons we cannot even understand. Whereas the short-term impact of AI depends on who controls it, the long-term impact depends on whether it can be controlled at all."*

Embroiled in unwinnable wars it knows how to start but doesn't really care to end, the U.S. clings to the two-party system, both factions the flip sides of the same tarnished coin, both indistinguishable one from the other except for the partisanships they create and the antipathies they inspire, both tied to corporate wealth, both committed to blocking meaningful reform in the name of Wall Street-controlled crony capitalism, both involved in larceny against the poor. Justice has been replaced by the aggregate interests of the dominant power base.

The gap between the haves and the have-nots continues to widen. The Catholic Church, the richest empire on earth and the self-appointed moral arbiter to millions, is embroiled in sordid scandals. Living in Babylonian splendor, basking in the idolatrous reverence of the flock, "princes" of the Church sneer at mankind's earthly struggles. Intoxicated by the apocalyptic rants found in Revelation, evangelical Christians yearn for an all-consuming Armageddon.

The crucifixion of Jesus of Nazareth is a fitting metaphor for man's inhumanity to man. Alas, its commemoration, in the aftermath of the Crusades, the "Holy" Inquisition, the Armenian and Jewish holocausts, the wars of conquest, liberation, and retribution, reminds us all that salvation—like justice, human rights, compassion, ethics and love—remains a distant vision, not a serious objective.

Nothing has changed. From the time of Jesus until the present, the world has been filled with violence and injustice, and Christians have shed more blood in Christ's name than all other peoples. In the 13th century, Genghis Khan couldn't recognize the world that Attila had conquered five centuries earlier. In the 1960s, George Edwyn Wolcott's grandmother, a child of the "Gay '90s," couldn't recognize the genteel New England milieu in which she'd been raised. This "disembodiment" from the dreary realities of the past is what drives some Earthlings to look at yesteryear with rose-tinted glasses while scuttling any prospect of a better tomorrow. They are the same sanguinary creatures they were then. Only some of the pretense has rubbed off. Educated, worldly, Wolcott's grandmother was astute enough to recognize that the differences are only cosmetic:

> *"People were as lustful and debauched and hypocritical and greedy and habituated to war when I was a young girl as they are now. They just dressed differently, put on prudish airs and rode in horse-driven carriages...."*

∞

In the past three decades, ongoing conflicts around the world have claimed more than four million lives. They continue to kill in Afghanistan and Syria, Colombia and Somalia, Mexico, Sudan, Libya and Iraq. Insurgencies and sectarian rivalries in

Southeast Asia, sub-Saharan Africa, and Latin America snuffed out another million lives. Five million more were lost during the Korean War; almost half that many in Vietnam. Displaced by war, famine, persecution, and poverty, some 50 million people were forced to flee their homes and have taken refuge in countries that are hard-pressed to absorb them, shelter them, feed them. The ongoing exodus is fueling resentment, cultural frictions, xenophobia, and racism.

History is written then retouched, tweaked. One man's truth is another man's propaganda. The allure of history rests not always on the events it chronicles but in the chronicler's subjective interpretations. Without these "adornments," the annals of man would consist of little more than a terse compendium of facts and dates. Whereas some social scientists tend to interpret history as an evolution from savagery to emotional maturity and intellectual refinement, reality is far less comforting. In the aggregate, human society seesaws wildly between states of stagnancy, feverish creativity, restlessness, turmoil, and madness. While these oscillations can be blamed on the cretins, killers and kleptocrats we elect (or surrender to), they are hastened, prolonged and fossilized by the appalling lethargy or rashness of the masses. Voltaire wrote: *"History is a lie commonly agreed upon."* Yes, victors write history to justify and exalt conquest, losers to mitigate defeat. Neither side will concede the other's account. The Turks deny exterminating a million or more Armenians; the Japanese continue to worship war criminals; 70 years after the fall of the Third Reich, some Germans still insist that the only mistake Germany ever made was to lose the war. These horrors are a reminder that the worst villainies are committed by those who falsify the facts and dehumanize their rivals.

∞

In a tale, as in a revolution, the most difficult part to invent is the end. Storytellers must not only have a flair for history, they must own up to it: An ending is not supposed to be a surprise. To envision the kind of ominous climax suggested in Khibxk's narrative—that creation's payback is extinction— readers must also reflect on the paroxysms of lunacy and violence that lend it credence, that are apt to hasten it. One facet of madness is the willingness to kill, or die, for an idea.

W. E. Gutman

All About Earthlings

POSTSCRIPT

The world continues to inch closer to doomsday. That's the message from the Bulletin of Atomic Scientists, which moved its iconic Doomsday Clock up two minutes on Thursday, January 22, 2015. In recent years, the clock has moved in the wrong direction for humanity. It now stands at three minutes to midnight, the "nearest" it's been since 1984, when the Cold War between the U.S. and the Soviet Union threatened to erupt in a nuclear conflagration. Said Kennette Benedict, executive director of the Bulletin of the Atomic Scientists:

> *"Today, unchecked climate change and a nuclear arms race resulting from modernization of huge arsenals pose extraordinary and undeniable threats to the continued existence of humanity. And world leaders have failed to act with the speed or on the scale required to protect citizens from potential catastrophe. These failures of leadership now endanger every person on Earth."*

There is cause to believe that the penalties imagined in *ALL ABOUT EARTHLINGS* are worthy of the crime and may be long overdue.

William F. Wu